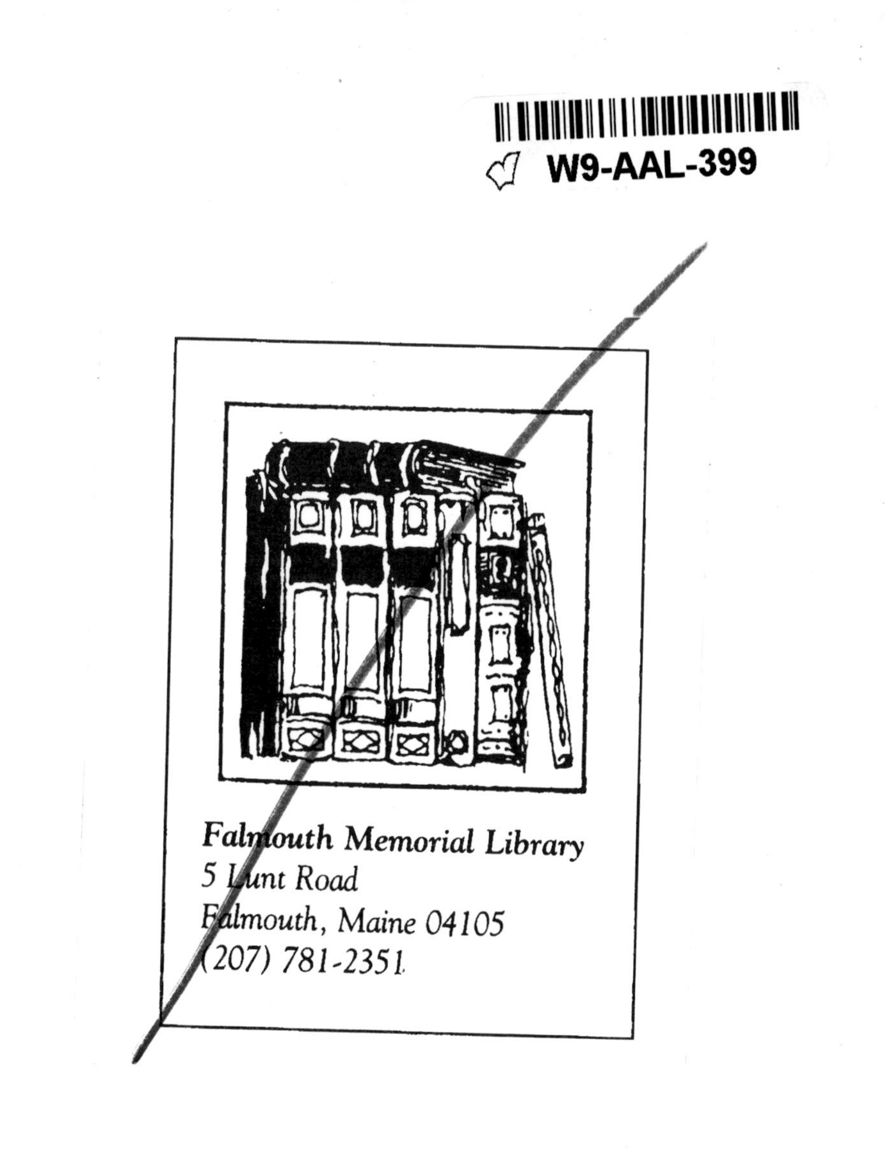

The Cabinet of Earths

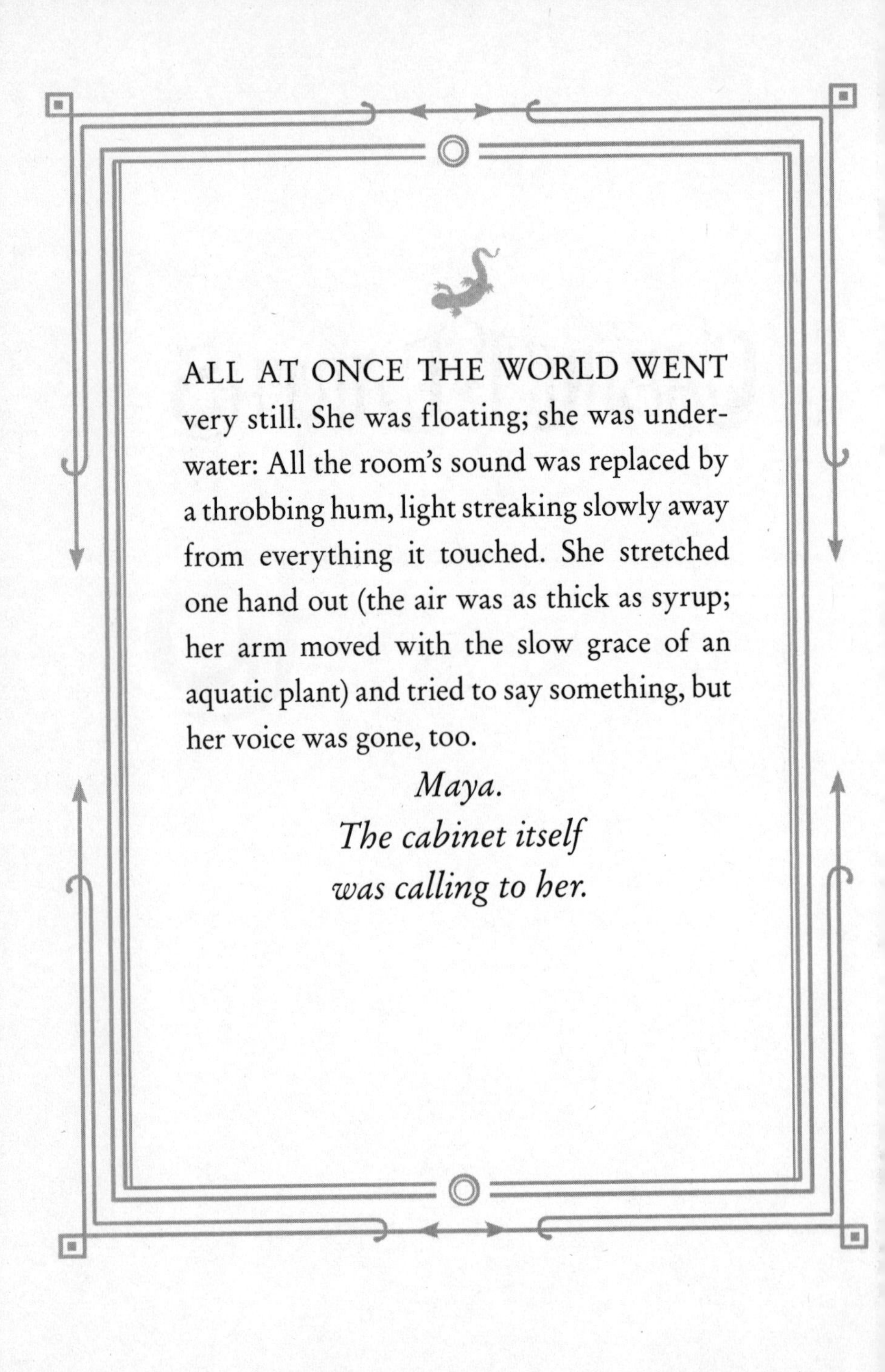

ALL AT ONCE THE WORLD WENT very still. She was floating; she was underwater: All the room's sound was replaced by a throbbing hum, light streaking slowly away from everything it touched. She stretched one hand out (the air was as thick as syrup; her arm moved with the slow grace of an aquatic plant) and tried to say something, but her voice was gone, too.

Maya.

The cabinet itself
was calling to her.

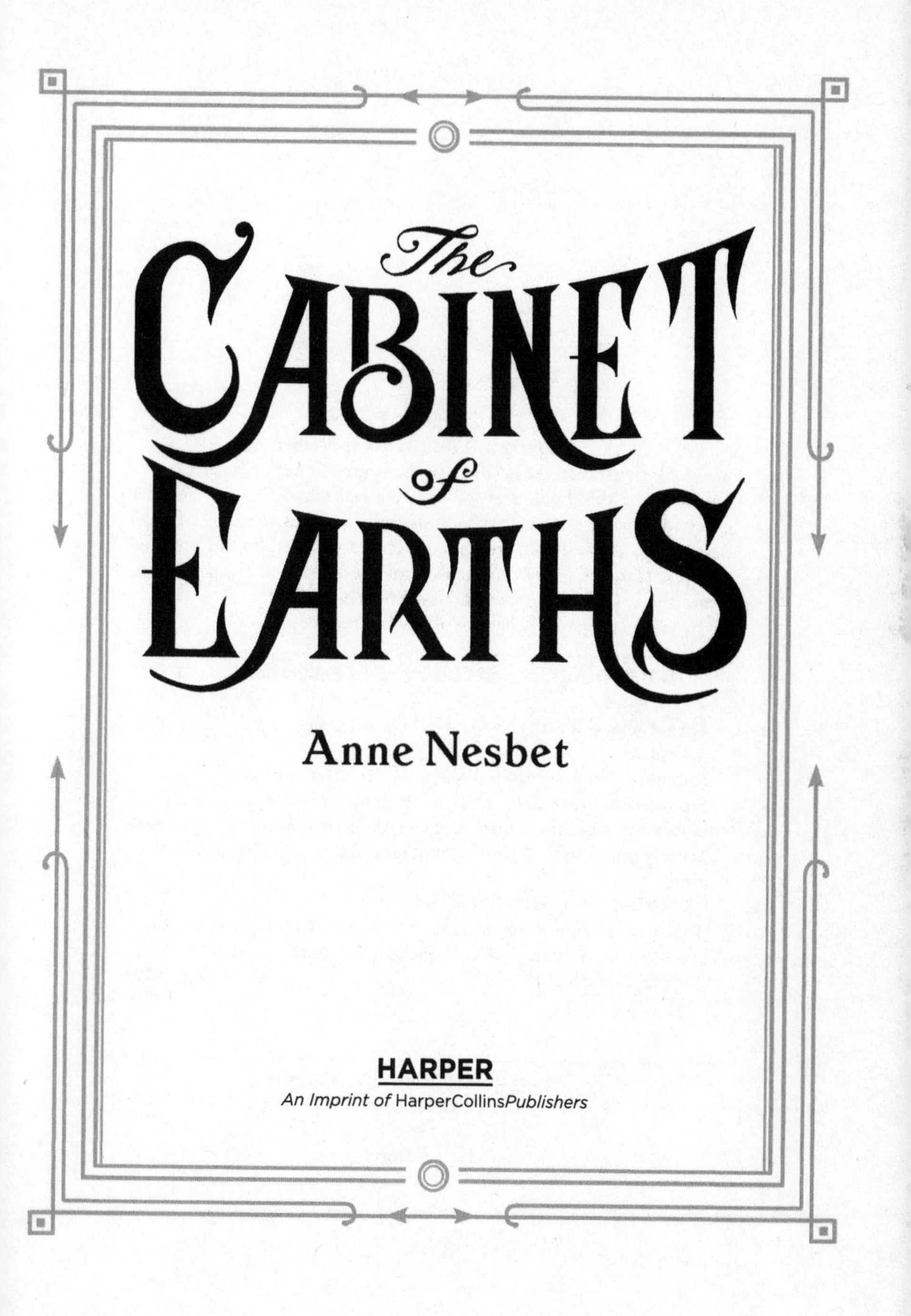

HARPER
An Imprint of HarperCollins*Publishers*

The Cabinet of Earths

 For information address HarperCollins Children's Books, a division of HarperCollins Publishers, 10 East 53rd Street, New York, NY 10022.
www.harpercollinschildrens.com

Library of Congress Cataloging-in-Publication Data
Nesbet, Anne.
The Cabinet of Earths / Anne Nesbet. — 1st ed.
p. cm.
Summary: Twelve-year-old Maya, in Paris with her family for a year, lands in the middle of the mysterious La Societé's quest for immortality when the magical Cabinet of Earths chooses her as its next Keeper, promising to restore her mother's health. Includes historical notes.
ISBN 978-0-06-196313-1 (trade bdg.)
[1. Magic—Fiction. 2. Immortality—Fiction. 3. Family life—France—Paris—Fiction. 4. Paris (France)—Fiction. 5. France—Fiction.] I. Title.
PZ7.N437768Cab 2012 2011019392
[Fic]—dc23 CIP
AC

Typography by Andrea Vandergrift
12 13 14 15 16 LP/RRDH 10 9 8 7 6 5 4 3 2 1
❖
First Edition

For Thera, Eleanor, Ada, and Jenna,
the girls of the Square de Robiac

CONTENTS

Nothing is lost, nothing is created,
all is transformed.
—Antoine-Laurent de Lavoisier

1

A TANGLED FAMILY

It was his own grandmother who fed Henri-Pierre to the Cabinet of Earths, long ago when he was only four. Don't misunderstand! It happened like this:

They were dark and cold, the first days of 1944 in Paris, and between the winter and the war, everything was bad. There was never quite enough to eat, and the rooms they lived in were never really warm, but when the electric lights winked out, Henri-Pierre and his grandmother lit a candle and huddled around its friendly yellow glow, feeling almost comfortable despite everything.

"Hands are for making things," she told him. Her own were slim and nimble and had magic in them that could turn an odd end of wood into anything you asked for: a tiger, a salamander, a tiny ship with paper sails. Once upon a time those hands had helped make the Cabinet, and the Cabinet was maybe the most beautiful thing in the world, with the mysterious bottles glimmering behind its glass front.

"What do we keep in our bottles, little one?" she asked him sometimes, and he would make the wrongest of guesses, just to hear her laugh: "Lemonade! Water! Tea!"

"Not in *our* bottles," his grandmother would say (their own private joke), and she would lean forward and whisper the secret into his ear: *"In our bottles we keep Time."*

So Henri-Pierre knew what Time must look like: black grains of earth, straining like something hungry against the bottle glass.

"It wants to get out," he said once, and his grandmother moved him another pace away from the Cabinet (which he must never, never touch).

"Yes," she said. "The earths will always dream of the people they came from; that's true. Time is restless that way. It wants to live in things and change them and make them old."

She put an arm around his shoulder and leaned closer, to whisper right into his ear.

"But in our family we know: There are secret ways to hold time."

"By *magic*," said Henri-Pierre contentedly. It was like the glow of warm milk in your belly, the knowledge of all the things your grandmother could do.

His grandmother surprised him by shaking her head.

"Not just magic, little one," she said. "Someday you'll understand. Oh, I walked in magic every day as a girl, but what did I know? It was how we saw the world, my family: my mother, my grandmother, all of us. Walking in magic is not *using* it. But your grandfather came and found me—"

"—And brought you away from the woods and the fields," said Henri-Pierre, in a happy singsong. (He had heard this part of the story many times.) "And brought you to the city where the towers grew—"

"Yes," she said. "The largest tower of all had just grown there, and your grandfather had helped build it. Because in *his* family, they were always scientists: builders and chemists. And *he* was a real Fourcroy, handsome as a prince and twice as ambitious. A great man, your grandfather! He said to me: *Think what we can do, the two of us together! Science and magic, in a wonderful tangle!* A tangle, you know, is more powerful than a single thread alone."

Henri-Pierre had had snarls in his hair, so it was hard for him to think of tangles as something very grand, but he nodded anyway, like a good child, to keep the story going.

"What he began, we continue," said his grandmother, and for a moment she seemed too splendid to be anyone's grandmother. She seemed like someone who should sit on a throne and rule a whole country, not huddle in a cold room in Paris with a little boy like Henri-Pierre. "We have an hourglass now—not here, my dear! hidden away!—that can pull the earth right out of a body. Yes. And the earths stay safe in their bottles, and the Cabinet holds them, and their people, wherever they are, can never grow old or ugly or die. You see how fine a thing it is, child, to be a Cabinet-Keeper!"

She smiled when she said that, a smile that danced like fire in her lovely eyes. She was the best and kindest of grandmothers. And that was not all: She looked so very young, almost like a girl.

The war had taken his parents away. Fever had killed his mother, and his father was in what they called (in whispers) the Resistance, which meant fighting and hiding and never being able to come home. Only his uncle came by sometimes, his beautiful uncle with the purple-blue eyes.

"*Beautiful!*" His grandmother had laughed at him. "Is that how we speak of our uncles, Henri-Pierre?"

But his uncle *was* beautiful. When he walked along the streets of Paris holding his beautiful uncle's hand, people turned their heads to watch them go by.

And then one day the terrible letter came, and when his grandmother looked up from it at Henri-Pierre, her eyes were like two dull stones.

"Your father is dead, Henri-Pierre," she told him. "My

son is dead. And his own brother is the one who betrayed him. So my son has killed my son."

He couldn't understand what she was saying, but the look on her face frightened him very much.

"Your *beautiful uncle*," she said, and the words were as cold as the metal bars of his cot. "Not so beautiful, after all! I find I want no more part of this world."

She got up from the table and went into the other room where the Cabinet was, and Henri-Pierre followed her on his little quiet feet.

He was still very small, so when his mind stored this day away as a memory, it may have changed some things or even made things up. Because what happened next was very strange indeed.

His grandmother lit the two big candles on the table—and then went up to the door of the great Cabinet in the corner and put her hand right through the glass. He must have seen that wrong. Right through the glass front of the Cabinet went her hand, but the glass didn't break. Instead it swirled a little, like a pond when you throw a stone into it. It rippled. Inside the Cabinet the candle-light flickered in the many glasses there: the tall flasks, the little vases, the clear, fluted bottles. Even the earths themselves, in their glassy containers, seemed to wake up to the candlelight, to give off sighs of color: red, brown, ocher, yellow.

He saw his grandmother's lovely hand hesitate for

a moment, and then close around one of the Cabinet's bottles—her own bottle! she had told him that once, which bottle was hers—and bring it out through that swirling, liquid glass.

"Oh, *Grand-mère*, don't!" he said, because he knew the Cabinet must never be touched, and there was something horrifying to him in the sight of her fingers emerging from that vertical pool of glass.

She put the bottle down on the desk and turned to look at him.

"My poor child! You are so young, but I'm afraid it must come to you," said his grandmother. "I trust no one else, and the Cabinet must have its Keeper."

What exactly happened then? He must have stumbled. He fell forward into her arms and felt something sharp pierce his hand, so that the blood came welling up, and his grandmother took that hand and pressed it into the glass of the Cabinet, only it really wasn't proper glass anymore. It was something else that crept like melted wax around his small fingers, flowing and strange. For the briefest of moments it felt like something was being torn from the deepest part of him. He cried out, and at that very instant his grandmother pulled him away from the Cabinet, and the glass was whole again and solid.

Long after, the pictures would come back to haunt him: his grandmother at the table with her bread—and everything covered with the eager, shifting grains of earth she had poured out of that bottle of hers, the bread covered with earth, earth spilling out of the cup she drank from, earth creeping toward the corners of her lovely mouth, while he stood there and pulled on her arm and cried.

"How well it remembers me, the earth!" said his grandmother, as if it were all a dark wonder. As if it didn't matter that a child was weeping at her elbow, wanting her to stop all this and be herself again. "After all these years, it comes back to me. Good. I want to be done with everything." And that was the most frightening thing he had ever heard.

He pulled on her hand, her familiar, gentle hand, and as he touched it, it changed under his fingers, became wrinkled and dry and splotchy.

"*Grand-mère!*" he cried out, but something terrible was happening to her face as well, her lovely, loving face. The light was fading in her eyes, the smooth skin of her cheeks becoming wrinkled and brown.

"Oh, my dear boy," said his grandmother, noticing him again. She was sorry for him; he could hear the pity in her words. "Cry for your father now, yes, but don't waste your tears on me. Not yet. Even this way, I will last a little while."

But never again did anyone mistake his grandmother

for his mother: no. The earth had stolen her beauty and made her old, all at once.

"She lost her son," they said about his grandmother, "and her hair went white overnight. Like a fairy tale, the poor thing."

Well! It is better to read fairy tales than to find yourself caught in them. His grandmother had withered away, and the Cabinet's spell had pierced the soul of Henri-Pierre: His body and spirit were curled up tightly around it, and it would not let him go.

Henri-Pierre de Fourcroy grew up and grew old, waiting for someone to come who could break that spell and rescue him. More than sixty years he waited, and then he woke up one morning and felt a twinge in his bones: change in the air. He did not know it yet that summer morning, but the person he had been waiting for all these years had finally come to his country, and the wheels were in motion that would bring her to his door.

Her name was Maya Davidson, she was twelve years old, and she had spent much of the month of August in a very bad mood.

2

THE SALAMANDER HOUSE

That sneak of a mirror was what gave her away, lurking as it did in the little lobby between the main entrance and the inner glass doors leading to the stairs and the elevator. It was dim in the lobby, and Maya (trying so very hard to be helpful and cheerful) was hauling the umpteenth suitcase in from outside when a shadowy figure caught her eye and made her jump. An actual French person! What would she say! But at that very moment her dad slapped a button, and the lights came on, and she saw it was only her own worried face staring back at her, caught like a prisoner in the glass of the wall-sized mirror. Like a strange, sad creature in a cage at the zoo. There should really have been a little label under the mirror to complete the effect:

MAYA DAVIDSON, 12. HUMAN GIRL.
NATIVE TO CALIFORNIA.
NOW FOUND ONLY IN CAPTIVITY.

Which all goes to show that it is hard to hide how you feel, when mirrors are out there everywhere, just waiting to pounce.

"Hear that?" said her father. "That brother of yours is *already* making a racket."

It was true. Some small elephant was galumphing down the stairs from the apartment four flights above, shouting loud, silly things as it went: "Ticky! Ticky! Boo!"

Her dad stuffed another two suitcases into the tiny elevator and called up the stairwell.

"*James!* Hush! Your mother needs some quiet!"

A pair of curtained doors burst open, and a large woman, her hair in a bun on the top of her head and one hand planted in warning on her hip, came glaring into the lobby.

"*Monsieur!*" she said, but it was Maya she frowned at—and then she went on and reeled off a page's worth or more of angry French. You didn't have to know a word of the language to understand perfectly well what she was saying: *Elephants in French apartment houses—not allowed! Noise of any sort at almost any time—not allowed! American children—*

At that point James himself, no longer an elephant at all, came through the door into the lobby, and the woman swiveled her head to look at him.

"James, this is Madame Pascal," said Maya's father.

And James smiled and put out his hand, for all the world like a child who has done nothing but study the international rules of etiquette for years on end.

The concierge melted, of course. Adults always did, when confronted with James, the bear cub look of him, his tawny brown hair, his brown, brown eyes, the dimple in his left cheek, the way he looked right into their suspicious faces and smiled. Everything that Maya had to steel herself to do, like asking strangers for directions or talking to the person in the next seat on an airplane, came as naturally as breathing to her baby brother. And he was only five!

While the woman started another speech in French, this one in an entirely different tone of voice (*"How cute your son is! How adorable! How well-behaved"*—again it was easy enough to understand the gist), Maya added a suitcase to the crowd of bags waiting for their turn at the elevator. They looked like such patient little creatures, those suitcases. It almost made her smile, despite everything.

"No shoving, now," she told them, and turned to go back for the next.

It was one of those moments: the concierge retreating, her irritation apparently all evaporated, back into her den; James beginning to bounce up and down on his heels and pulling on Dad's sleeve; her father's face slipping for a moment into the tired worry that was always there somewhere these days. Thinking about her mother, probably. Thinking about noise.

"James!" said Maya. "You know you can't be loud in here. Let's go outside and look around."

"Exploring!" said James. "Cool!"

Her father looked so relieved that Maya almost felt embarrassed.

"Oh, yes, good idea," he said. "That's my girl! I'll finish up here. Wait, wait—here's a map of the *quartier.* Look, I'll make an *x*—that's our building. And right there—that's James's school. Go give it a look, maybe, you and the Live Wire—"

Who was already pulling her right through the door.

"Let's go over there," said James, pointing down the street with his free hand.

"No, no, it's this way," said Maya, finally having found their street on the map. "You heard Dad. We're going to go look at your new school."

"Soon I'm going to have about a hundred new friends," said James, with total confidence. "And they're all going to be French."

"Well, good for you," said Maya, and the bitter wave of thoughts that overtook her then—going to *school* in this place! in *French*! with *no friends at all*!—made her drag James along down the street so firmly that he yelped in protest.

"You're pulling my arm off!"

"No, I'm not," said Maya. She did slow down, though. They had come to a pretty big intersection, and then it looked like they were supposed to go on up the next avenue, the one that went at a strange angle to everything else.

"Well, you don't have to be such a grump face all the time about it," said James.

A flash of misery went right through her. Her mother had a saying for bad days: *Life is full of lessons, and the grades aren't fair.* By which she might as well have said, *Sometimes your mother gets sick*—really sick, like having to go through chemo and losing all her hair and most of her get-up-and-go—*and you have to be a very good sport.* Not just for a day or a summer, but for *years.* And here are the lessons Maya had learned about trying to be always, always a good sport:

1. it's exhausting; and
2. nobody notices; and
3. it doesn't really work very well, anyway.

Nope. Because consider this. When Maya's mother was finally done with chemo and radiation and all that other awful stuff and tiny curls of hair were beginning to sprout up again like lamb's wool on her bare head, she had looked up from dinner one night and said in this funny voice, sort of wistful and hopeful all mushed up together:

"You know, Greg, I was thinking again about Paris."

There was a laboratory in Paris that wanted Maya's

dad to come do research there. Physical chemistry, which was his particular specialty. A letter had even come from a society of some kind, all gold seals and long words—a special fellowship so he could bring his whole family! Moving expenses! An apartment!

"Almost like magic," said Maya's mother.

"No such thing as magic," said her father, the scientist. "But it's pretty good news anyway."

And then her parents both turned and looked at Maya.

And at that moment Maya's fate was sealed. Because let's face it, when your mother, your one and only mother, whom you love more than anyone else in the world, has come back from nearly dying of cancer to say that her one great wish has always been to take the family to France for a year—you do not say no.

You say, at most, "Umm . . ." And a few months later all the muscles in your face will ache from trying to form the helpful, positive expressions *good sports* wear on their faces all the time, and you will find yourself standing on the avenue Rapp in the center of Paris, five thousand miles from your best friends and your bedroom and your *dog*, and despite all that effort all that time, every mirror you glance into will echo back your miserableness at you.

She blinked away the tears as roughly as she could, and at that moment James yanked himself free from her hand and ran forward a few paces.

"Look, Maya! It's a salamander on the door!"

James was very into salamanders, because they were amphibians.

"No, it's not," said Maya, without even bothering to look, and then she did look.

"Hey," she said. "I take it back. That *is* a salamander."

It was large and made of brass, and its head was turning to look at them. It was, in fact, the handle of the front door of that house, the one right in front of them. What kind of building had a salamander for a door handle? Maya stepped back to look.

It was one of the strangest buildings she had ever seen. It was covered with patterns and carvings—iron phoenixes decorating the edges of the door, a beautiful, melancholy stone woman staring down at them from above the door, a fox draped gracefully about her neck, more people farther up—were those Adam and Eve?—plants, the heads of cows holding up a balcony on one of the upper floors. And almost every line a curve of dark stone. Swirls and curves, like waves breaking or vines coiling.

James had his head pitched at an impossible slant, the better to stare up at that complicated, swirling façade, and then he started to laugh.

"Look, it's you!" he said. "They put a Maya statue on their building!"

"Don't be silly," said Maya. "That's not me."

Her head was beginning to hurt. It had been such a long, strange morning. She squinted up at the building, and the sad stone woman gazed right back down at her, her carved eyes full of secret stone thoughts.

"My hair's not that long," said Maya, but she almost didn't finish the sentence. It was true—there was something familiar about that face. Too familiar, almost. She backed away another step or two, taking James with her.

"It's *you*," said James, with total conviction. "Cool!"

Was that really how she looked? Couldn't be. But then again, maybe she *would* look something like that, if she were carved from limestone or granite or whatever it was.

A stone mirror, she thought. And felt, for a moment, most peculiar.

"Let's cross the street so we can see the whole of it," she said, her voice just a bit too loud in her ears.

The building was not symmetrical; that was part of its oddness: About three floors up, a rectangular window on the left contrasted with a tall, curvaceous oval on the right, as if the building were raising a skeptical eyebrow. And above that, a narrow balcony lined with pairs of pillars in another kind of stone, something green and mysterious. It was another world, that building, and that other world was gazing down at them as they stood on the corner with their heads cocked back.

"There's a man up there looking at us," said James, pointing. "See him?"

"Don't stare," said Maya, grabbing James's hand again.

"He's the one staring," said James, and then he smiled and waved up at that vine-green balcony, those undulating, gazing windows.

"James!"

Really, it was impossible, trying to keep him under control. She looked up quickly, trying to assess the damage, and caught a glimpse of a dark-haired man leaning over the little balcony way above, something dangling from one relaxed hand: glasses? a pipe? She had had enough. She swung James right around to get him back on track, facing down the other little street, the one his school was supposedly on.

"It must be right here," she said, her jaw tense. And then: "Oh, whoa!"

Because when they turned into that street, all they could see for a moment was a lacework of iron climbing high, high into the sky.

"It's the EVIL TOWER!" said James, delighted. "Is this my school? Wow! Look at that! The Evil Tower is right above my school!"

"Eiffel," said Maya. "It's the *Eiffel* Tower."

The strange thing was it didn't look like any postcard of Paris she had ever seen. It was much huger than she had thought. It was really, really big. It was immense. And the building on the left really was an elementary school. But James could hardly be made to glance in the school's direction. His eyes were stuck like glue on that tower.

"Can we go up to the top?"

"Not now," said Maya. "It's time to go back, anyway."

"Let's go right up to the top!"

"I said, not now."

She practically had to drag him backward to the avenue Rapp, his head all tilted with longing as the Evil Tower fell away out of sight behind his future school. They had to wait at the crosswalk for a moment then, just opposite that strange house with the salamander on its door. You could not help staring at that door. It was so alive with creatures and curlicues, and when the door swung open, the salamander looked back over its bronze shoulder at you in the most disconcerting way.

No, not just that: It looked right at Maya and flicked its thin, bronze tongue.

Maya jumped and blinked. So that was what jet lag could do to you! Make door handles come alive!

But then the man who had just come out through that swinging door across the street paused to adjust his glasses with his long, pale hands, and for a moment Maya could see no salamander at all.

"Look!" said James. "There he is again. That's him!"

"Don't point," said Maya, her heart still racing a little from the weirdness of the salamander.

"I wasn't pointing," said James. "I was waving."

"Don't wave either!" said Maya, in some haste. "It's a rule: You can't wave at people you don't know."

She said that very quietly, bending down over James's ear and kind of blocking his view with her arm for a second, just because you never knew, with James, when he might start not just smiling and waving but—who knows?—handing around invitations to his next birthday or something.

"It's green!" said James, unperturbed. He had been peeking under her elbow at the light. "Come *on*. Did you see his dark goggly glasses? I bet he's a spy."

The man couldn't have heard. He was all the way on the other side of the street, after all. But he paused for a second and turned his head very slightly to the right, just as a person might turn his head to listen to some interesting sound coming from fairly far away. And then he straightened up and walked away, his steps fluid and bouncy. Young steps. He was a very young man, despite the elegance of his clothes.

He strode down the avenue Rapp ahead of them, turned left at the corner, and disappeared.

"Now we can go," said Maya, giving James's hand

another squeeze. It was the strangest thing: There was something about that elegant young man, about the graceful way he sliced through all this soft Parisian air that made a person want to run along after him for a while, just to see where he might be going. There was something about him that drew you to him, that made you want to see more of him, that might even (if you were James's age) make it very hard not to smile and wave. Maya could see that was the case. She could feel that call of his in her very bones.

But it made her think for some reason of the magnets they show you in science class, bars of metal all furry with iron filings, paper clips, or nails, and the thought made her stubborn all over again.

She and James were not paper clips, were they? She made her feet go extra slowly for a moment, just to give the elegant young man time to get well ahead of them and away.

Just beyond the strange house with the salamander on its door was a little blind court of a street, and more curlicued stone, and what looked like the entrance to a theater, of all things. THE ALCHEMICAL THEATER it called itself in elegant stone letters above a pair of large doors: What kind of theater was that? The smaller letters underneath didn't make things any clearer: THE SOCIETY OF PHILOSOPHICAL CHEMISTRY, they said.

"Boofer would really like Paris," said James thoughtfully, eyeing the elegant stone corner of the Alchemical

Theater. "There are lots of really great places for dogs to pee."

And then there was a *boulangerie*, which Maya knew meant a bakery, and an antiques store, and some other sort of business, and then a café across from the strangest fountain, all stone cherubs and banners, and by that point her feet were moving fast again, eager to get back to her parents and the apartment on the fourth floor in the rue de Grenelle that would never, never, ever quite be "home."

"First you drag, and then you rush!" complained James. "I wanted to go up to the top of the tower!"

It was just as they swung around the last corner and their own doorway came into view that the strange thing happened.

The door opened and out stepped—

"Him again!" said James, and before Maya could think of anything to say or, alas, manage to grab his hand, James was already erupting into a big smile and a wave—

—at the same elegant young man, his hands once again adjusting the fit of the dark glasses he wore.

They were really *very* dark glasses.

And at this moment those dark glasses were turning right toward Maya and James.

"Ah!" said the young man. It was the sound of someone rather pleased, for private reasons, by what he now saw. *"And here,"* he said, *"must be the children!"*

He said it in French, of course, but Maya could

understand every word of it. They weren't very hard words. What she couldn't understand, however, was why a stranger in Paris would be staring at her and James at all, much less exclaiming as if in recognition, and much, much less coming out of the door of the very building where the Davidsons were going to live.

"Well, well, well," said the stranger, while one of his long pale hands patted the other in an absentminded way.

"Perfect," he said. "The boy and the girl!" Pause. "Indeed, most charming!"

And then the man nodded, turned, and walked away so fast that one otherwise unremarkable woman coming the opposite way was nearly bowled right over in his wake.

A cold shiver went flying through Maya's limbs. What, after all, had the man from the Salamander House been doing *here*?

"Come *on*," she said to James, giving him one last impatient tug.

Because suddenly all she wanted in all the world was to be already up those four flights of stairs and within sight, reach, and earshot of her ordinary, lovable, thoroughly unmysterious parents.

3

OUR FAMOUS COUSIN LOUISE

"Well, there you are!" said their father as he came out onto the landing. The rattly old elevator gave a squeaky shudder and began to crawl noisily back down to the lobby. "How does Paris look? You know you've already missed our first guest."

"The spy," said James. "We saw where he lives. There's a salamander on his door. When can we go up to the top of the Evil Tower?"

"Excuse me?" said their father. "Spy? Salamander?"

"That man with the dark glasses," said Maya. "We saw him downstairs. James thought he was a spy because of the—"

"Oh, I see!" said their father with a laugh. "Of course. Quite logical, James. But I'm afraid he's not a spy. Something wrong with his eyes, probably. Odd fellow—from that Society, you know. Must be the youngest Director any Society ever had. Seemed very disappointed to have missed you kids. Kept asking about you, and then off he went."

The elevator clattered to a halt, four floors below their feet, and there were various knocks and bangs as someone sidled into it.

"What Society?" said Maya.

"Actually, he didn't miss us," said James. He had sat right down on the doormat to wrestle with his shoes. "He saw us downstairs."

"They gave me that fellowship, remember?" said their father to Maya as he held open the door. "So that I could bring you all along for the year. The Society of Philosophical Chemistry—I think that's what they call themselves. Hurry up, James, let's get off the stairs. And this apartment, too—it's theirs."

The creaks and rattles were getting louder again: The elevator was nearly there.

"I bet maybe that's the spy again," said James happily.

But when the door of the elevator opened, nobody in particular came out. Not a spy, not a Director of any Philosophical Society, just an unremarkable sort of woman looking for some other door.

"In we go, then, kids," said Maya's dad, in a quieter voice than before, and he nodded in the direction of their hall.

There was a nondescript sound from the landing. And

then another, but they weren't the sort of sounds that leave a mark on the brain. And in any case, Maya was still busy with the thought of men in dark glasses and apartments that somehow mysteriously belonged to them and their shady Societies.

A hand was tapping her on the shoulder.

"Excuse me," said the unremarkable woman, for the third or fourth time. "Would this be the *appartement* of Madame Sylvie Miller Davidson?"

Maya did turn around then and looked at her, or at least tried to. She was strangely hard to see. No color to her, somehow, just an oddly muted effect, as if there were a curtain of frosted glass between Maya's eyes and her. Or a kind of haze in the air, almost. Just an ordinary sort of woman, but too vague to be properly ordinary, because *ordinary* ordinary people become more vivid when you pay attention to them, and this woman—well, you couldn't quite focus on her, somehow.

Madame Sylvie Miller Davidson! It sounded so strange in the woman's mouth, so bland and so foreign, both at once.

"That's my mother," said Maya.

"May I ask—" said her father.

"I wrote to her," said the woman. "I said I would be coming, right away. I am," she added, "her cousin."

And then she somehow trickled right by them, in

through the door, and down the hall.

"My goodness," said Maya's father in a slightly weak voice. "At this rate, we'll have had forty-eight guests by Friday."

Maya slipped under his arm and through the door.

"Like clockwork, one per hour," he said, shooing James in after and shutting the latch carefully behind him, without the slightest bang. "But perhaps the pace will slow at night?"

"Shh," said Maya. What had traveling done to her eyes? The salamander on that strange building had turned its head and flicked its brass tongue at her. It couldn't really have done that—but it had. And now this woman who had just walked past them and down the hall: How could an ordinary person be so very hard to *see*?

In the living room, Maya's mother was already rising from her chair and listening to something the woman was beginning to say in that voice that sounded so oddly like nothing at all.

"How kind of you to come," said Maya's mother with great earnestness, as if the vague person in front of her were a Nobel Prize–winning duchess or a terribly famous poet, instead of being—well, whatever she was. Less notable than people usually are, somehow. "We've all wanted to meet you for such a very long time. Maya and James, come say hello. Can you guess who this is?

This is our famous Cousin Louise!"

James looked skeptical.

He said, "But Cousin Louise was a–"

"Come shake hands," said their mother. But James was not to be deterred.

"*—baby,*" he said with great definiteness. "A baby. That's what she was! Ouch! You're pinching me!"

Maya tried to quench him with a look, which didn't work at all, and then she gave up on subtlety and angled herself in between her brother and the vague figure of Cousin Louise, whose blurry hand was perhaps already reaching out to her, though it was somewhat hard to tell.

She had eyes that were an ordinary dull sort of brown. Her hair was almost no particular color at all. And when Maya took her hand, she felt–*all right, this is strange*, thought Maya–she felt *nothing*. Do you know how your cheeks and tongue and lips sometimes feel, after a trip to the dentist? That was what it was like, shaking Cousin Louise's hand. It was like the little bit of the universe containing Cousin Louise made everything around it just slightly numb.

"Enchanted," said Maya in at most a wobbly whisper. *Enchantée!* That was what you were supposed to say when meeting French cousins. Even if they were really quite the opposite of enchanting. That's how French is.

She was only distracted for a second, but it was long

enough. James wriggled by, picking right up where he'd left off.

"You were only three," he said, with some relish. "And the church crumbled down all around you, and you became *famous*."

"Well, now," said Cousin Louise.

Maya gave her a worried look, but on that plain, unreadable face there was no sign of annoyance, not a trace of pain. No trace of much of anything at all, as far as Maya could see.

In fact, maybe nobody on earth ever seemed less like someone famous than the Davidsons' famous Cousin Louise. She was exactly the sort of person that when the whole sixth grade is heading off to the old Victorian mansion of John Muir, and there's going to be an hour-long bus ride to get there, and everybody's chatting and sorting themselves in that awkward way that happens before you get on the bus—well, Cousin Louise is the kind of person you end up sitting next to, when you'd really rather not. And then it's up to you, of course, not to let the poor person next to you know how much you are half-listening all the time to the fun the people a few seats behind you are having, and so really the whole bus ride is a bit of a chore.

"I bet it was scary," James was saying. "Was it really, really scary?"

"I'm afraid it's entirely my fault he's pestering you,"

said Maya's mother, leaning forward in her chair. Her face was pale, but her eyes were very alert, the light dancing in them the way it tended to do when something had caught her attention. "I've told them the story a thousand times, you see. They've seen the newspaper articles and the pictures. I hope you're not offended."

"Offended," said Cousin Louise, quite blank. "Why?"

There was a little hiccup of time in the room, during which Maya's mother offered everyone cookies, and everyone but James politely refused.

"Well," said Maya's mother brightly, as if starting over again. "I'm so glad we've finally found you! And my mother would have been so glad. She wanted to adopt you, you know, when . . . when . . . that terrible thing happened, when the church fell down and everybody was killed, even your poor brother—"

"Your poor brother was Nicolas," said James solemnly. "He was six. And the church was made of *stone*."

"Oh, dear," said Maya's mother.

But Cousin Louise still had not so much as flinched.

She said instead, in her dry and plodding way, "The children, I presume, will be going to school?"

School! Maya's heart closed around that word like a sea anemone poked by an unfriendly hand. School! And while her mother rattled on about the forms they had filled out, and the various educational establishments in the *quartier*, and her conviction that being thrown into the French public schools would, in the end, be the best experience her children could ever possibly hope for, Maya thought about home, and the new locker she would have had if she had stayed at Livingston Junior High where she belonged, and the way her friend Jenna would again this year almost certainly bring her stuffed chipmunks to class on the first day, just because that was what Jenna always did at the beginning of every year since the first day of kindergarten five million years ago—and she forgot all about Paris for a moment. Just closed her eyes and remembered what it felt like: school!

But then Cousin Louise said, "*Mais oui*, of course," and that brought Maya right back out of her daze. She had just managed to miss something important. What?

"How wonderfully kind!" said her mother. "Maya, how about that? Cousin Louise has just offered to help you with your French."

There were, in fact, audible underlines under all of those words. Maya's inattention must have been showing.

"Oh, Mom!" said Maya in horror, and her father, who believed in the comforting effect of treats, pressed a cookie into her hand.

"Of course we don't want to inconvenience you, Louise," said Maya's mother. "There's your work."

Maya looked up in hope. But no—

"Bah, the work," said Cousin Louise. "I file letters,

papers, forms in the basement of an enormous firm. Anonymous labor. They will not mind me, present or not present. I am *invisible*."

And for a moment there seemed to be almost a flicker of something in Cousin Louise's eyes. Perhaps only Maya saw it, that quick winking of light, and Maya looked away very fast, feeling a little strange inside.

She knows, thought Maya, keeping her eyes well away while her stomach did that odd, embarrassed flop. *She knows what she's like.*

When Cousin Louise had finally said *au revoir*—which means, unfortunately, not just "good-bye" but "until we meet again"—when she had disappeared, neither smiling nor frowning, into the rattly old elevator and gone off and away, Maya's father leaned back against the apartment door for a moment in mock exhaustion.

"No more," he said. "I don't care who it is; I don't care what Society they run; I don't care whose long-lost cousin they may be—that's it. We don't open the door."

"Well, I was glad to meet her," said Maya's mother, relaxing a little into her chair. "And now Maya will have help with her French."

A wave of frustration sloshed over Maya's edges at that. And she was so tired, too! Your edges always get sloshier when you're tired.

"But, Mom," she said. "Don't you see what a crazy idea that is? You don't know anything about her. For all you know, she could be an *ax murderer*!"

Maya's mother looked distinctly taken aback.

"Good grief, Maya," she said. "Louise is our cousin. She's not an ax murderer."

"Even ax murderers are *somebody*'s cousins," said Maya. "She's a little strange, couldn't you tell? She's, like, blurry or something. Didn't you *notice* how strange she is? I can't go wandering around Paris with Cousin Louise. She's practically invisible."

Maya's father laughed out loud.

"Slow down!" he said. "Just because a person's not, um, especially memorable—"

"Not that," said Maya—to her mother, not her father, because if anyone was going to understand about statues on buildings that looked like you, and brass salamanders that came alive when you walked by, and cousins that were surrounded somehow by a blurry, numbing cloud, it would be her mother. "I mean really, like, *invisible*. Couldn't you see that?"

For a moment Maya thought she saw a spark of recognition lighting her mother's eyes—"*You, too?*" said those eyes for a millisecond—and then the millisecond was over, and her mother blinked, and whatever that light had been was forgotten and gone.

"Maya," said her mother kindly. "Calm down. Think of it this way: It will be good for Louise, having some contact with her cousins."

Maya was just opening her mouth to say—something!—when her mother stopped her with the tiniest shake of the head.

"Look," said her mother. "Brains are very delicate things. You know that. Do you think her life has been easy? An injury like that can change someone's entire personality."

Maya's mouth stayed open for another moment, and then she gulped it shut.

"Injury?" she said. "You mean, she was hurt?"

"Maya!" said her mother. "A whole church fell on her!"

("With a great big CRASH," said James, from somewhere under the table.)

"But," said Maya. "You didn't tell us she got *hurt*."

She was beginning to feel pretty foolish. Of course, it made sense. All that rock tumbling down! And then never to be the same as you were before that happened! It was an awful thought, to tell the truth.

Though something naggled at her about it all. She remembered the picture. It was in the album back home, a clipping from the newspaper, as old as could be. The smiling child in the arms of her rescuers. Grainy smile, grainy ruins, big headline shouting something in Italian underneath, because they had all been tourists in Italy, Cousin Louise's family, when the church fell on them.

Just the slightest flutter of a thought—*smiling!*—and then it winked out again and was gone.

"It's probably something along the lines of autism," said Maya's mother. "Though she wasn't born with it. Anyway, I know you'll handle things with your usual good sense. And now—"

She yawned.

"—I'm taking a nap. Go look at your room, James, why don't you? It's right down the hall. . . ."

There was a long moment of silence in that apartment, still so empty and unfamiliar, with the suitcases scattered around like toppled bricks. For the first time, Maya noticed the wall of the living room wasn't a straight line at all, but a long curve. Even the windows had a curve to them, and through the rippled glass she could see the street winding along and the windows of the building just across the way, with their fancy iron balconies good only for potted plants, not people. And slate-colored roofs with more windows thrusting out from them. All in all, the place looked remarkably like, well, Paris.

"Where's my room?" James was asking from farther and farther away. "Here? Is this it? Can I mess it up now?"

She ran her fingertip along the curving wall, all the way to the fireplace in the corner, where there was a potted plant at one side and a mirror above, tilted just the tiniest bit, so that her own face looked down at her, her eyes darker in the glass than they usually looked, darker and more serious, somehow.

And then when her finger got as far as the mantelpiece, it tripped. There was the smallest paper corner of something, trapped between the mantel and the wall. You could see that someone had painted over the joint where the mantelpiece met the wall, but not very carefully, and there was a black line of a crack visible now. And that was where her finger had tripped: not on the crack itself, but on a tiny cardboard corner that stuck out from that crack, no farther than a fraction of an inch. An eye might not notice the bump of it, even, but a finger did.

And her fingers were already working carefully away at that corner in the crack, easing whatever it was out, bit by bit, trying to get just enough cardboard between her index finger and thumb to pull the thing out. Because if she lost hold of it now, she saw, it would fall all the way into the depths of that crack and be gone for good.

Maya was good at fiddling things out of tight places, though.

With a slight sigh of paint dust, out it came: a large envelope, quite old, it seemed. With something in it. Several somethings. They poured out easily into her hand: photographs. Black and white, square-shaped, odd. *How old they must be,* she couldn't help thinking, *these pictures of children in quaint tailored coats and antique sweaters. Walking along sidewalks, looking up into the camera with a smile and a wave: alive, almost.*

Almost alive.

She was tipping a photograph back and forth in her hand, watching it shimmer.

A little girl, maybe four years old, with dark ringlets spilling out from under her tam; dark, sparkling eyes. Sparkling. Yes—

"So what've you got there?" said her father. Out of nowhere, almost. Maya jumped.

"Bunch of photos," she said, hugging the envelope closer to her chest. But she held out a hand, to give him a look.

"Hnh," he said, an appreciating sort of sound. "Cute kids. Used to live here, maybe. Nice old prints, too. Different emulsions back then, you know."

Then he drifted back out of the room again. Suitcases trumped photographs.

For a while, however, Maya could not move away from that place or look away from those pictures. They were silvery in a way she had never seen a photograph be silvery before; almost three-dimensional, somehow, when you rocked the shining children in your hand. Not everything in those photos had that magical fullness: The trees, the sidewalks, the cobblestones in the background stayed flat, and even the other figures in the frame, the passersby, the extras.

But oh, the beautiful, luminous children!

Those children were like little flames of silvery depth flickering against the ordinary flatness of everything else, and some of the flames were brighter and deeper than others.

On the backs of the photographs were neat notations in pencil, numbers followed by something that looked like a droopy “X”: “174_X,” “56.8_X,” and even “216_X!!” on the photograph of the ringletted girl.

“Adèle,” it said there, in fine and feathery script, and a date she could not read. 1951, maybe. 1957?

Maya’s breath caught in her throat, and her fingers tingled as she slipped the photographs back into the envelope they had been waiting in all this time. It was the strangest feeling that filled her now, after all that long day of travel, bronze salamanders, elegant young men in sunglasses, and cousins your eyes just slipped right over—

She felt—really she did!—as if the very walls of this room had sent her a letter.

4

THE BABY WHO SANG IN THE RUINS

They had just slogged through Parisian puddles for an hour, and now Cousin Louise was looking up and down the street, choosing a café.

"There," she said finally, with a point and a sniff. "We'll go there."

She liked cafés. Well, in principle, Maya did, too. Sitting at a little round table in Paris, watching well-dressed people stride by in their high-heeled shoes, *clickety-clack, clickety-clack*, while you sipped a fizzy drink—nothing more relaxing than that, under ordinary circumstances. That is to say: in other company than that of Cousin Louise.

"Please request that table over there, Maya," said Cousin Louise (never in English, always in French). "The one facing the fountain. I'll have a *café crème*, very hot, please tell him."

Even in parts of the world where people speak English, it can take some gumption to tackle a waiter on a busy day. But every afternoon spent with Cousin Louise led like clockwork to this uncomfortable moment when Maya had to sort through her new French phrases, fingering them like foreign coins in a pocket to see what she had to spend; when she had to march forward and catch the eye of a man whose vest and apron meant business; and then had to *galvanize herself*, open her mouth, and talk.

This time Maya's face must have sagged into a frown for a moment, because when they were safely at their table, and the waiter was about to bustle back any moment with their drinks, Cousin Louise asked, "You think I am making you do this only for tormenting you?"

(Maya could understand more of Cousin Louise's French now, but her brain still made peculiar English of it.)

"*Non, non,*" said Maya halfheartedly.

"But listen, Maya," said Cousin Louise. "If I ask for a table, I will not get one. If I order *café crème*, they will not bring it. They do not see me."

For a moment Maya was filled with the most peculiar thought: *Maybe that was the literal truth!* Had she spent this week trailing a truly invisible person all over Paris? But what could that possibly mean? What if the whole Davidson family was simply being *haunted* by this Cousin Louise?

It was a foolish, impossible thought, but still she had to

put her hands in her lap to keep the worry from showing, and when the waiter came with the drinks, she watched him with an eagle eye. But he put her Orangina and a tall cylindrical glass on her side of the table and the coffee on the other side, quite as if he realized Maya was not there all alone. A relief. Cousin Louise might not necessarily be a ghost, after all. Which would have been awfully hard to explain to her parents, come to think of it, if it had turned out to be true.

"So," said Cousin Louise, after testing the temperature of her coffee. "And how was it, the first day of school?"

But of course she used the French expression: *la Rentrée*. The Comeback. The Reopening. The Return. The words don't work so well if you're a refugee from California and deeply missing all your friends and your dog.

Maya thought about her day, about how during *récréation*, which was recess, all the normal students stood around looking cool in their black jackets and chatting in French, while the friendless new kids hung out on the edges and, if they were Maya, counted the many, many days remaining before the next vacation. And decided it was safer to talk about James instead.

"My brother seems to be doing very well," she said. (Taking the usual pauses before the verbs.) "He bounced to school this morning—is it all right, 'bounced'?—with his new backpack and his new pencils. And this afternoon he bounced out once more, very contented. He likes school."

Not to mention that three or four little boys had waved good-bye to him as he took Maya's hand to walk home.

"I see," said Cousin Louise. "It is easier for him. He is not at all invisible, that one."

Maya stole a look at Cousin Louise's inscrutable face and then gave her soda a determined stir. The thing was, even when Cousin Louise seemed to be making a joke, you could never be quite sure enough to laugh.

"Yes, he will take taxis all the time, if he wishes, when he is big," said Cousin Louise, as if that were the measure of something grand. "He will hold out his hand, and they will not speed by. They will see him and stop. They will even serve him coffee when he requests it, in cafés."

She rested her bland eyes on Maya, in whose mind those taxis and waiters had gotten all tangled up with the black-jacketed crowd at the Collège Paul Sabatier. Being ignored? Well, even Maya knew something about that.

"And now," said Cousin Louise, opening her book. "We will talk about the *imperfect past.*"

As if the present weren't imperfect enough! At least in the past there had been friends to hang out with, and a dog that loved you, and a world that spoke your own language.

But Cousin Louise meant a verb tense. About which

she went on and on and on. Maya was trying her best to pay attention, but her mind kept drifting away to more interesting things: the brightly lit windows of the shops, the little fountain with its sad cherubs holding up their marble banner, the tourists sauntering by with their cameras dangling from wrist straps and their noses buried in their guidebooks, the flock of fashionable students making a smooth and languid turn into the entrance of the café, like the birds swooping from tree to tree in the Champ de Mars.

"*Aux enfants perdus*"—the café was named after the fountain. "What children?" thought Maya drowsily. "Lost how?"

"Maya," said Cousin Louise. "Maya!"

Maya gave a guilty start. She was pretty sure that Cousin Louise had been trying to get her attention for some time already.

"I see you are indifferent to verbs today. But if you would be so kind as to catch the waiter's eye."

Just at that very moment, though, someone gave Maya a friendly tap on the shoulder.

"Hey there," said a boy in English, very close to her ear. Maya jumped in her chair and twisted around to see who it could be.

"I think you're Maya," he said. "Excuse me. Aren't you?"

He had dark brown hair, almost black, the slightest

hint of a curl in it. And eyes that were a surprisingly friendly gray. But why was a random boy calling her by name? In English? In Paris?

"Whoa, sorry, didn't mean to startle you," said the boy, holding out his hand. "I saw you at school this morning. The new girl from the U.S., so I was curious. Maya, they said."

"Maya Davidson," said Maya, shaking the boy's hand. He had appeared so suddenly that she didn't even have time to feel shy. "You were really at that school? You're American!"

"No, no," said the boy. "Actually: Bulgarian. But, you know, I lived in New York for four years, so . . ."

He shrugged and smiled.

Maya couldn't help smiling herself: the first honest smile to cross her face since who knows when.

"Why were you in New York?" she asked.

"Parents are diplomats," he said. "So then they got posted to Paris. Too bad for me! Had to start all over again. Tons of fun."

"What's your name?" asked Maya.

"Valko," he said. "Means 'wolf.' V-A-L-K-O. That's how they spell it here, anyway. In Bulgaria it's different. Are you here for good?"

"Oh, no," said Maya. "Just a year. My dad's working in some laboratory."

"How's your French?"

"I'm working on it," said Maya. And then remembered. "Oh, yes! This is my Cousin Louise."

Valko looked rather taken aback for a moment. Quite the way you'd look, in fact, if an empty chair turned out, on third glance, not to be empty, after all. He shook Cousin Louise's hand with an apologetic smile. And then looked puzzled.

Oh! thought Maya. *Maybe he feels it, too!*

But you can't just up and ask someone if his hand has gone numb. Not with Cousin Louise right beside you, more or less.

"Delighted," said Cousin Louise, everything about her, as ever, nondescript. And faded back into her chair.

"Well, then," said Valko, hesitating for a moment. He kind of gathered himself together to leave—a moment of decision—and then pulled a stool over from a neighboring table and sat down instead. Maya found she had been holding her breath; she let go of it with a flustered cough and scooted over to give Valko some room at the table.

"I was in your shoes a year ago," he said to Maya. "That's why I wanted to say hi. I know what it's like. I've been new a million times. It gets better, really it does. Some of the kids at school are all right. Of course—"

He gave a quick nod toward the other end of the café, where the flock of stylish students had clustered around a boy with very well-combed hair.

"That's the Dauphin," said Valko. "His crowd, I would avoid."

"Dolphin?" said Maya.

"Dauphin, not dolphin. Eugène de Raousset-Boulbon—that's his name. He comes from a family of Beautiful People. No, wait, I'm not kidding. You should see his parents. They look like they're about twenty-five years old. Do your parents look like they're twenty-five? Nope, mine neither."

He gave his left palm an expressive jab with his thumb.

"Local aristocrats, that's what," he said. "Secret societies and fancy clothes. Seriously! What the heck is 'Philosophical Chemistry' supposed to be? It's not really chemistry, because chemistry is science. The Beautiful People have nothing to do with *science*. They don't like foreigners, either. I'd stay away; that's what I advise."

"So why is he a dolphin?" asked Maya. Inside her head, the words were still humming: *Philosophical Chemistry*? Like the building? Like the people who had brought all the Davidsons to Paris?

"Oldest son of the king, that's what a dauphin used to be. Not related to the sea. Not like fish. Thinks his daddy's the King of Paris or something. Well, never mind them."

He laughed.

"Really, though, welcome to the most uneventful

quartier in Paris," he said. "Except for the occasional abducted child"—he waved at the fountain—"nothing has ever happened here, and nothing ever will."

And then he looked at his watch, gave another friendly nod, and took off down the avenue with the quick lope of a wolfhound.

Rosalie, 1951; Amandine, 1954; Laurent, 1955; Adèle, 1957—missing, but not forgotten, said the sad cherubs' banner, as Valko retreated into the distance beyond it. *Edouard, 1959; Marie-Jeanne, 1960; Stéphane—*

"And have you much homework tonight?" said Cousin Louise, whom Maya had again completely forgotten for three or four minutes—not just forgotten the way we forget our parents when their presence might be a problem, but *forgotten entirely*. If Maya had been a bus driver, she would have driven right past her without a second thought. It chilled your bones somehow, thinking about what it must be like to be so forgotten, all of the time.

How could a church falling on your head do that, make you *forgettable*?

But that reminded her of something. She had thought about it last night as she was brushing her teeth. She had been watching her face in the mirror and thinking about photographs, and then this other thought had come and sat down, like a stubborn dog, in the middle of her brain.

"Cousin Louise," she said. "You were smiling in that

photo, the one we have back home."

It was not unlike talking to a wall, or a haystack, or an empty chair. But the thought wouldn't budge, so she plowed gamely on.

"The photo from the newspaper," she said. "It's in an old album my grandmother had."

"Excuse me?" said Cousin Louise, looking at her as if from a long way off.

"From when the church fell on you. There's a picture from when they dug you out, and you're smiling and waving your arms—"

Cousin Louise made a vague sound, but she did not interrupt.

"And the headline says it was a miracle. Mom translated it for us. And they found you because—because—you were *singing in the ruins.* You were almost a baby, but you were singing, and they could hear you, and they could see you, and they pulled you out, *safe and sound.* That's what it says."

This time Cousin Louise made no sound at all. Just sat there, like a blank space, waiting for something.

"It's just that Mom said you were hurt by the church," Maya said at last, all that silence making her cheeks burn with awkwardness. It had seemed important, last night in the bathroom. But now—

The blank space that was Cousin Louise shifted a little

in its chair. And sighed. And began, after all, to talk.

"Well," said Cousin Louise. "A *miracle*. Now that is very strange. Because I am sure something happened to me at some point. An accident. Damage done somehow, all the same. I don't know. A question for that uncle, I suppose, if I can find him."

"What uncle?"

"The one who took me in first," said Cousin Louise. "After the accident, you know. I have no memory of him, but I know his name: Henri de Fourcroy. They sent me to so many different people when I was a child. Nobody wanted to keep me. I made them uncomfortable, even then. They are made uncomfortable, you know, or they do not notice me at all."

"My mother said it was like autism, what you have," said Maya, surprising herself. It wasn't like her, to blurt such things out. She almost clapped an anxious hand to her mouth. But Cousin Louise didn't seem perturbed. She just shook her head.

"Autism? *Non*. Not that," said Cousin Louise. "I have read about that. How the minds of others can be opaque, they say, to people with autism. Probably I describe it badly. But that is not the case with me. No—"

It was just so difficult to keep herself focused on what Cousin Louise was saying. Maya was trying very hard, and still her mind was straining at the leash, like Boofer on a walk, whenever a squirrel would come dancing across the road.

"—The inverse of autism, Maya," Cousin Louise was saying. "I myself am opaque, for some reason. Their eyes cannot see me. Yes, that's it: The world is autistic with respect to me. There! Pay this waiter, and we will go."

She stood up, almost too suddenly. Maya blinked.

"Yes, come along!" she said to Maya. "Because I think you are right: If not the falling church, then what can it have been? You will look him up in the phone book, if he is still alive, and we will go ask him those very questions. Come! We are going to find this uncle, you and I, this *Henri de Fourcroy.*"

5

THE CABINET OF EARTHS

They found him tucked away down an alley off the old rue du Four, in the very center of Paris. *Henri-Pierre de Fourcroy*, it said on the mailbox at the street door. *Second courtyard, ground floor.*

"You can say that you're a cousin, visiting from America," said Cousin Louise, as they followed the passage back into the hush and the shade. "True enough, yes? Tell him that."

The second courtyard was small and crooked, the cobblestones very rough underfoot and the walls rising up all around them slightly green with age and dampness, as if, with another few days of rain, they might just sprout right out in a thick layer of moss.

And along the back wall, the lower section of one of the buildings sprawled out into the courtyard itself, a fantastic construction of wood and windows that looked like something James might love—the perfect tree house—though here it hugged the ground, far from anything even resembling a tree.

"Here it is," said Cousin Louise, who had been examining the courtyard's various doors, and as she spoke, the door itself squeaked open. A man's wrinkled head peered out at them, all worry and suspicion. His hair was thin, tufty, and gray, and his eyes a shy and watery color.

"*Oui?*" he said, in a voice made slightly crackly by age. "Who are you? I take no more deliveries, you understand! Not from Them!"

Cousin Louise stepped very slightly to one side, her sign that Maya should do the speaking for them. As usual, Maya had to let go of a slight feeling of irritation—of put-upon-ness—before she could get down to the hard work of stringing French words together.

"*Bonjour, monsieur,*" she began, a safe way to buy some time. "I don't know who Them are—" (She knew right away that she had messed up the grammar; a faint click of disapproval came from the general area of Cousin Louise, on her left.) "—But I am Maya Davidson, from California. And I think we are cousins."

Somewhere above their heads a pigeon added some mournful comment of its own: *Oo, oo. Ooo-oo. . . .*

"'Cousins,' you say?" said the old man, in a wondering sort of way. "I have no cousins."

"Not a *close* cousin," said Maya, wondering how one

really said any of this in proper French. "Distant. Far away. My grandmother was French."

"Oh?" said the old man. He looked rather puzzled. "Well, what was her name?"

"Anne-Sophie," said Maya. "Anne-Sophie Miller."

"But I have no Millers in my family," said the old man (and of course in his mouth it sounded like this: "*Meellaihr*"). "I'm afraid you must be mistaken, *mademoiselle*."

"She means *Lavirotte*," said Cousin Louise, in her bland, gray voice. The old man looked up at her, almost in alarm, and then looked away again.

"Lavirotte," he said. "Ah."

Of course, that was right. Maya felt foolish all over again. The French grandmother had had a different name before she married Maya's American grandfather and moved away.

"But then—" he said, and peered at them with, if anything, renewed suspicion. "You are sent by the *Société*, after all? I told you very plain, did I not? 'No deliveries,' I said. I still say it. I am done with all that."

"What Society?" said Maya. "Deliveries of what?"

"BOTTLES," said the old man, a deep frown furrowing the lower half of his wrinkled face.

Maya felt a giggle bubbling up in her throat, but the old man seemed so very earnest about it all that she worked very hard to keep the giggle under wraps.

"I promise we don't have any bottles, Monsieur Fourcroy," she said. "Really, truly."

"Not sent—you're quite sure—by the Society—?"

"No!"

"—of Philosophical Chemistry?"

The bubble of laughter inside Maya vanished just like that. Evaporated. Popped. *The Society of Philosophical Chemistry!* The same Society that had given her father all that money so he could bring them along to France? And paid for their apartment? And had a rather riveting young director who lived in a house with a salamander on the door? Was there any corner of Paris free of them?

All she could do was shake her head, while that trickle of surprise danced up and down her spine. But the old man seemed not to notice. In fact, he was already stepping back to hold the door open for them.

"Well, come in, then, I suppose," he said. His face had softened, all at once, into the shy ghost of a smile, a curious smile. It made him look almost like a boy, for all that his skin was so wrinkled and his hair so sparse. "My grandmother was a Lavirotte, yes, when she was a girl."

There was an odd vestibule just beyond the door, with a couple of old winter coats hanging on pegs and a weather-beaten umbrella propped up in the corner.

And through the doorway to the left, again another

world: rows of large windows (for this was the earthbound tree house, seen from the inside) letting in the light of late afternoon, and rough workbenches covered with tools and materials, and everywhere boxes, the most extraordinary boxes, filled with tiny chairs and people in strange costumes and animals and books the size of a thumbnail and cups and mirrors and things Maya could think of no name for.

"Oh!" she said aloud, her eyes and mind entirely amazed. "Dollhouses!"

She had never cared very much for dolls, exactly, but miniature things she had always, always loved. Once, long ago, her mother had taken her to a museum filled with dollhouses, and Maya had stood in front of those miraculous tiny rooms and felt herself falling into them, everything about her ordinary life unsettled for a moment, magic slanting into her world like an odd beam of light. And here were perhaps more of those dollhouse rooms than any museum could hold. There were extra shelves built into the walls to hold them; even the workbenches and counters overflowed with boxes. A hundred different universes in a single human-sized room.

"*Mais non,*" said the old man, full of pride. "Not dollhouses! Sets!"

"Sets?" said Maya.

"Why, yes!" said the old man. "I am a *décorateur* for

the theater. These are scenes from the opera, *mademoiselle*. Not dollhouses."

"You make sets for operas?" said Maya.

Operas were such large things: large people singing large arias in extremely large and velvety halls. It was hard to imagine all that largeness coming out of the little boxes hidden away in this back-courtyard room.

"For one particular opera," said the old man. "*The Chemical Brothers*. My life's work, you understand: the tragic tale of the Fourcroys. How that curse settled on them, on us, long ago. See? I have been all morning making sheep."

And it was true: One of the worktables was covered with fluffy little sheep in various poses. The box next to them had a waiting green felt field unfurled across it, a tiny man in a small but elegant suit of gold cloth gesturing toward all that green as if saying, "All very well. But where are my *moutons*?"

"An opera about sheep?" said Maya.

"Ah, *non*," said the old man. "One brief rustic scene. That man there, observing his sheep? He was the one we killed, we Fourcroys. The great man of science, Antoine-Laurent Lavoisier. You have heard of him?"

No, Maya had not.

"The construction of the table of chemical elements? The theory of the conservation of matter? The battle against alchemy and superstition?"

Maya shook her head.

The old man looked distressed.

"The guinea pig in the ice calorimeter?" he said, in a smaller voice. "You've heard, perhaps, of the guinea pig?"

In the next box, two itty-bitty men were indeed placing a tiny fluff ball of a guinea pig into the strangest apparatus, a kind of miniature double tub with blocks of plastic ice between the inner and outer walls.

"Slow-burning fires in us," said the old man, so close to her ear that Maya jumped. But he was just peering over her shoulder. "That's what they learned from the guinea pig. The year 1780, my dear. They measured the little furnace in him by the ice he melted. We are all little furnaces! Oh, yes! But the great chemist Lavoisier was the first to measure it properly. He was a true scientist, he was!"

"Very nice," said Maya politely, but really she was thinking that an opera about chemistry might not be very entertaining to sit through. Even assuming you liked operas at all.

"The great Lavoisier," said the old man, oblivious. "Father of modern chemistry. And we—we!—killed him. It is very sad, but true. All explained in the third act, you know, of *The Chemical Brothers.* Over here, dear girl. Come see!"

More boxes. A courtroom scene, with judges hanging

over their benches to waggle their cotton fingers at a small man with bound hands. Another figure stood to the side and turned his back. And in the next box, a sad line of men, their heads bowed, waiting for death beneath a miniature guillotine.

"There they are," said the old man, almost whispering in his enthusiasm, as if not to disturb the little characters in their boxes. "The great Lavoisier, condemned by the Revolution in 1794—and his fellow chemist, his brother in spirit, Antoine-François de Fourcroy, who turned away from him, you see—who betrayed him!—and let him go to his death. Oh! Here they sing both at once, but very different songs. The most terrible moment in the whole opera, *mademoiselle.* But beautiful, oh, my dear one—beautiful indeed."

"Fourcroy?" said Maya. "Like you?"

"My great-great-great-great-grandfather, yes," said the old man, adjusting the crook in the tail of a tiny cat curled up beneath the scaffold. "A traitor, I'm afraid, to the ideals of both science and friendship. An ambitious man. Preferred power, in the end, to the pure gaze of science. We carry that betrayal in our bones, his descendants. Cursed to repeat it. I speak too plainly, perhaps."

"Not in the least," said Cousin Louise, from a few feet away.

"Oh, right!" said Maya, suddenly remembering again why they were here, in this workshop full of small worlds in boxes. "Excuse me, *monsieur,* but could I ask you a question? Not about chemistry or opera, though. About 1964."

He stopped and blinked at her.

"It's my Cousin Louise," said Maya, gesturing back toward the dull shadow of Louise behind them. "She lost her family in 1964. In Italy. A church fell down on them. Do you remember this? And then an uncle offered to take her, Henri de Fourcroy. But that's you, isn't it? Did you try to adopt my Cousin Louise?"

He was so lost he looked for a moment like a guinea pig must look, when it has spent ten long hours shivering in an ice calorimeter.

"Adopt?" he said. "Italy?"

"No, Maya," said Cousin Louise, moving forward from her place in the shadows. "I'm sure, having seen him. He is not the one."

And at that moment a tea kettle started to wail in an adjoining room.

"My tea," said the old man. "Excuse me. Would you like—"

"Yes, please," said Maya. She said this because Cousin Louise was about to insist that they leave, and they could not leave, not with this old Fourcroy, nobody's uncle after all, looking so lost and confused and forlorn. A shred of stubbornness had come to the surface just then, in Maya, and she was not going to leave until she had done what she could to put things at least somewhat right.

In fact, she was so intent on not letting Cousin Louise drag her away too soon that she followed the old man right out of his workshop through a door in the back wall, Cousin Louise trailing behind. The rooms on the other side of the door were old but ordinary rooms, very bare after the clutter of the workshop out in front, pictures on the wall, an antique table and chairs, a carpet on the floor, and in the corner—

"Oh!" said Maya. Maybe, in fact, she said nothing aloud at all, just stood stock still and stared, while the old man shuffled on ahead into his ancient kitchen.

In the corner of the room was a glass-fronted cabinet, the glass very old and ripply, thicker slightly at the bottom of the panes than at the top, and within that cabinet—

Bottles and vases, stoppered jars. Glass within glass, and in each of those glasses, a different vivid color of earth: reds, russets, browns. Glass bottles of earth on glass shelves in the glass cabinet. Around the bases of the bottles were odd shards of rock, with what looked like fossils peeping out, and broken stones that held crystal caves in them or that might have been meteorites that fell long ago from the sky, they seemed so old and black and alien.

The bronze frame of the cabinet, which seemed to

contain all of these marvels with the grace of a goblet holding some fine and transparent wine, was itself a wonder, a flowing ornament twining around all that rippling glass, a phoenix arching around one low corner, and there, staring down at her from the upper right—

"Don't touch! Don't touch!" cried the old man, almost dropping the tray holding the teacups.

—was a salamander.

All at once the world went very still. She was floating; she was underwater: All the room's sound was replaced by a throbbing hum, light streaking slowly away from everything it touched. She stretched one hand out (the air was as thick as syrup; her arm moved with the slow grace of an aquatic plant) and tried to say something, but her voice was gone, too.

The bronze salamander looked at her and smiled.

Maya, it said.

In their bottles, the earths glimmered and pulsed. Maya tried to blink, but her eyelids were very slow and stupid.

Maya.

The cabinet itself was calling to her.

Maya.

And then, all in a rush, the air was air again, and time was running at its normal pace, and Cousin Louise was saying something in her spectacularly ordinary voice.

"—But glass is also a liquid, I've heard," said Cousin Louise, as she took the tea tray from the tremulous arms of Henri-Pierre de Fourcroy. "Given time, it flows, however hard it may seem to be."

The old man made a strangled sound behind Maya's back. But Cousin Louise stood still, with the tray, as impassive as ever. Maya hardly knew what to say or where to look. Her skin was prickling all over with embarrassment and discomfort and some other, less describable feeling, as if the cabinet itself had somehow reached out and marked her. A tingle of electricity in the air.

"Oh!" she said, stepping back quickly. "I'm sorry! But what is it? What's in it? It looks like sand in those bottles. Or earth."

"Yes," said the old man, plucking at her sleeve with one trembling hand. "The Cabinet of Earths. And I am its Keeper, since ever so long. Don't touch. Not to be touched. Come away, now, please, *mademoiselle.* Come away, please."

But I didn't touch it, thought Maya in confusion as the old man led her away. *I'm sure I didn't. It touched me.*

So they retreated into his workshop once more, and Cousin Louise poured them all cups of slightly musty tea.

At first they were silent, the only sound in that cluttered, marvelous room the faint and unsteady click of the old man's spoon against the rim of his teacup. Maya's thoughts were one big mishmash of glass cabinets and salamanders and churches falling down and little fluffy sheep waiting to take their places on a green felt field.

The old man had dropped his spoon and was staring at Maya, as if his mind had just now finished working some very complicated calculation, and had come up with "*this girl right before you*" as the answer; Cousin Louise, having served the tea, was looking in no particular direction at all.

Maya took another bitter gulp of tea and set down her cup.

"*Monsieur* Fourcroy," she said. "What—"

But she found she could not ask about the Cabinet, not out here in the light, not with Cousin Louise taking delicate sips of tea just a few feet away. Maya's mouth would not form the words, and then her breath refused to bring them to life.

"I don't know what it means!" said the old man, a deeper note (awe?) now running through his voice. "I'm not sure! But I think—"

He leaned closer.

"I think it knows: It is time for a change. I have been here nearly seventy years. I am tired! I do not take deliveries! Not anymore! And you, my dear, are a true Lavirotte. An only child, I hope? If I may be so bold as to inquire."

Maya choked very slightly on her tea.

"I've got a little brother," she said, puzzled. "He's five. Why?"

"Oh!" said the old man. His face sagged a little, almost as if he had taken a blow. "Then be careful. It runs in the family, you know: Brother eats brother. It's a tangled family, ours. There's danger there."

"I don't understand," said Maya, by way of understatement.

"Why should you? You are young, and I've been sitting here all my life, making sense of it all. My grandmother, you see, was a Lavirotte, *ma fille*. Like you."

He paused to examine Maya's face for a moment, as if it had just now come properly into his view.

"*Very* like you! Ah, no wonder, then, that the Cabinet wants you. That you came to us, after all this time. I was trying to explain—"

Cousin Louise sniffed. But quick as Maya whipped her head around to look, she could surprise no ghost of emotion on that face, not even impatience.

"She had one brother. You must be the children of that brother, you, *ma fille,* and—and—"

He had forgotten Cousin Louise's name, of course; a weak gesture in her direction, and then he went galloping back to his family trees.

"Well, now, the Lavirottes! They have always been, more or less, *amphibious.* Yes. They can live in anything: water, air, fire. Yes, yes, like the little salamanders.

Citizens of more worlds than one, you know. Guardians and keepers. And those are the Lavirottes, my dear. *They walk in magic,* my grandmother used to say. Do you see things, little cousin, that others do not see? That's the Lavirotte in you, seeing."

He smiled at Maya and then tapped his chest with a bony finger.

"But my grandmother married a Fourcroy. And *they* are always hungry, aren't they? For good and for ill. They call themselves scientists, but they killed Lavoisier. And then they claim to be his heirs! They want power; they eat it up. Science and magic—nothing wrong with them, one at a time, as you might say. But tangle them together for the sake of *power*—"

He shook his head slowly and sighed. There was the tiniest of pauses, and then he looked up at Maya with a wistful expression on his wrinkled face.

"You've really never heard of Lavoisier?"

"My father's a scientist," said Maya, so as not to be too discouraging. "He might know about him."

"And your mother a Lavirotte!" said the old man, widening his eyes. "Oh, dear! Oh, dear! More tangle!"

He did look awfully worried.

At that point Cousin Louise made an ambiguous noise, startling to anyone who, like Maya, had forgotten she was in the room.

"Well, we've certainly taken up a great deal of your

time," said Cousin Louise, rising from the worktable where she had just finished her tea. "If I may ask, then: You already lived here in 1964?"

The old man looked at her, confused again.

"You were younger then," said Cousin Louise. "But you were not my uncle. I'm quite sure of that now."

"Quite young," he said. "But working here already, yes. So much younger even than you, *mademoiselle*, when it chose me. Oh, I've never lived anywhere else, *non*. I can't leave the—"

And he gave a meaningful nod toward the back room, where the Cabinet was.

"You see how it is," he said. "I don't even go outside much, *mademoiselle*. To the store on the corner! Yes! That far and no more."

"I'm sorry," said Maya, and she was. This kind, scattered old man brought out something protective in her. There was some part of him that was so like a child, with his fantastic boxes and his shy smile; he might be slightly crazy, or even more than slightly, but she liked him, all the same.

"Thank you for the tea," she said. Cousin Louise was already moving toward the door. "It was kind of you."

"My little cousin from America!" he said, and smiled at her with his gentle eyes. "You will come back again, I hope. You will surely come back. Be prudent; be careful; take care! And now, good-bye!"

He leaned forward a bit to whisper to her: "I must return to my sheep."

The door closed.

They stood, Maya and Cousin Louise, in the twilight of the courtyard for a moment, hardly knowing what to say.

It was Cousin Louise who first took a brisk breath and started walking back down the alley, back toward Paris and the everyday.

"So that's that, then," she said. "*Definitely* not the one. A useless detour, no relevance to anything else."

But Maya remembered the strange smile of the salamander—and knew that, for her, something in the world had irrevocably changed.

6 THE EVIL TOWER

Maya was putting the glasses away in the kitchen a few days later, when a glancing ray of light twinkled off the rim of a cup and reminded her of something.

"Hey, Dad," she said. "Is it really true that glass is a liquid?"

"Aha!" said her father, looking up from his book. "Glass! Now that's a truly interesting subject. Fixed, like a solid, but disordered, like fluids. Some say—"

It was always a little risky, asking Maya's father questions about science.

"Not the super-long version, right, Dad?" said Maya. "It was just something Cousin Louise said the other day. And even the glass in the windows here, you know. It does look a little bit like something flowing."

"Well," he said. "If I recall correctly, people argued for years and years that the reason some stained-glass windows were thicker at the bottom than at the top was because the glass was slowly flowing downhill with time."

It was the old man's strange cabinet that came immediately to Maya's mind, with its thick ripples and waves. That was what Cousin Louise had been looking at when she said that odd thing about flowing glass. So Cousin Louise had been right?

"Nonsense, of course," said Maya's father. "Old wives' tale."

And then he went on to say more about *viscosity* and *crystalline structures*, but Maya's mind was elsewhere—she was standing again before that cabinet, and watching the shimmering earths in their bottles. There was something hypnotic about that image, like a mad doctor's swinging watch in a bad old film. And yet that was the part of the visit to the crazy old cousin de Fourcroy that she had been unable to say anything about, when she was telling her parents the story.

Sets for an opera about a long-ago scientist (and his sheep and his guinea pig)! Her parents had enjoyed that, it's true. And her father had definitely heard of Lavoisier.

"Father of modern chemistry!" he said. "Didn't know he'd lost his head, though. Very famous guy. Conservation of matter, right, Maya?"

Maya's father had a disconcerting way of assuming you'd been listening very hard in every science class you ever had.

"Um," said Maya. "Sure."

"Just means nothing goes totally *poof*," said her father. "A pretty basic idea, you'd think, but the consequences—"

"Poor old man," said Maya's mother, accidentally interrupting. But she was obviously thinking of Henri-Pierre de Fourcroy, and not of the poor headless Lavoisier. And then she had to pause for a moment to cough.

That was when Maya's father surprised them all. He had been rummaging around in his pockets, looking through his wallet. Now he held up a little card and waved it in the air like a flag.

"Aha!" he said, looking very pleased with himself indeed. "Sure enough: *Fourcroy*! Now, how about that?"

"How about what?" said Maya's mother. "What's that thing you're brandishing about?"

A business card, very simply engraved:

HENRI DE FOURCROY, DIRECTOR
SOCIETY OF PHILOSOPHICAL CHEMISTRY

Maya's stomach took a strange, slow ride toward her toes.

"You remember him," said Maya's father. "He came to see us, that very first day."

"Oh, yes, with the sunglasses," said her mother. "Attractive young man. And so he's another Fourcroy! I guess they must be everywhere. Maya?"

Sometimes an unexpected surprise can have a sort of

narrowing effect on the universe, like a funnel. Maya was peering down this funnel at that name, and her mind was running in feverish little circles: *Fourcroy! The Society! That cabinet! Fourcroy!*

"But why didn't you *tell* me he was a Fourcroy?" she said to her dad.

"Good golly," said her father. "Was it important? I forgot all about it myself."

"Maybe we're even related to him," said her mother, giving Maya a reassuring pat on the arm. "You did say we're related somehow to the other one, the old fellow, didn't you? Here, let's see what we can do—"

She had been working on a drawing, so her sketchbook was right there at hand. That was what Maya's mother was like: always a project underway. Even back when she was very sick, she had kept a notebook near her bed all the time, in case a picture got into her head and wouldn't leave.

So now Maya and her mother scribbled out a rough family tree, with lots of question marks hanging from its branches. In the end they figured that this old Fourcroy was maybe their second cousin, twice removed. Nothing closer than that, even if his grandmother *had* been a Lavirotte. For the other Fourcroy, the young fellow from the Société, there was no obvious spot on the branches anywhere.

It wasn't a very bushy tree. The American shoot went

as far as James and Maya, but there were no first cousins around to thicken things for them.

And a great branching of the French side came to a forlorn end in Cousin Louise.

"That family almost died out twice, you know," said Maya's mother. "Before the church fell on them, there was the war. They were deported, you know."

Only Louise's mother had survived the war. And then she had had a church fall on top of her! Life was definitely not fair.

"Do you want to keep this, Maya?" asked her mother, and she tore out the page from her sketchbook with a quick swipe of the hand.

From the sketchbook another picture stared up at them: a fountain, sketched lightly in blue pencil and now only about half inked in. Sad cherubs hoisting a banner: *Amandine, 1954; Laurent, 1955. . . .*

"That's the Fountain of Lost Children," said Maya. "By that café."

"Yes," said her mother. "Odd things from the neighborhood; that's my theme this year. Did you know that was all some big mistake?"

"Mistake?"

"I went inside the café to ask about it. You know I do like to ask about things."

She smiled at Maya, one of her quick, dancing smiles.

And Maya smiled back.

"Anyway, turns out there was about a decade where children were disappearing, or so they thought, and lots of hue and cry and fuss, and some benevolent association collected money for that fountain—'adorably hideous!' said the man in the café; they seem quite fond of it there, in a way—and then after it was set up, it turned out the children weren't exactly missing, after all! Can you imagine? Oh, they'd each wandered off, the way children do, for an afternoon or something, or been misplaced in a store for an hour by their aunties, and been reported as lost, but once you looked more closely into the thing, it turned out they'd all pretty much wandered home."

"How could everyone have been so wrong?" said Maya.

"Mass hysteria," suggested her father. "Very common. Happens all the time."

Somehow Maya did not think that eight whole children could be rumored to have been lost or abducted or misplaced for a whole decade without anybody noticing they had actually been perfectly fine all along. But her mother shrugged.

"Some of them, the families had moved away. Others apparently had problems of some kind. Weren't in regular schools anymore. Maybe the parents were ashamed. Anyway, the kids had slipped out of the records, one way or another. These things do happen."

"But the fountain's still there," said Maya.

"Oh, yes." And Maya's mother laughed. "The café had moved in by then! They fought tooth and nail to keep the fountain, accurate or not. So there it still is."

Look at it this way: If Maya vanished for a day or ten years from her spot at the back of every class at the Collège Paul Sabatier, no one would ever have felt moved to carve a sad cherub bemoaning the loss of *her*.

"Meh," she said to Valko a few days later, when he asked how her French class was going. "The teacher hardly even glances at me. It's like I'm invisible."

She thought of Cousin Louise then for a moment and shuddered.

"Teachers never notice the ones who don't cause trouble," said Valko. "When I was younger, I was noticed all the time, believe me."

He laughed a bit, a nice laugh, and Maya felt the specter of her possible Louiseness dissipate just a bit.

"Still, I'll never ever fit in," she said (but already more cheerful about it).

"*Very* possible," said Valko. "Likely, even. But you don't have to fit in to be okay. Believe me! I am the not-fitting-in world expert. I have *not fit in* in maybe five different countries so far. I am homelandless. I even make mistakes when I speak Bulgarian. But it's no big deal, not really. It's not the end of the world, right? It's okay."

He did look pretty convincingly okay, Maya had to admit, for someone dragged all over the world all his life. Even if he was losing his native Bulgarian. Which was kind of a scary thing, when you thought about it. Let's say you get dragged off to France, and then your parents for some reason just plain forget to go back home. When do your ordinary English words for things start to disappear? And what does that feel like, when you notice they're gone?

"Hey, and how's your little brother doing?" added Valko. "He never even had any French before, right?"

"Oh, *he's* doing great," said Maya. "He always does great. The teacher has already sent a note home practically thanking my parents for bringing him to France. He had tons of friends by the third day. That's just the way he is."

And then, to her surprise, she felt almost guilty. She really did love James, of course, with all her heart. After all, from a purely objective point of view, he was probably the most lovable child in the world. Really. But then she opened her mouth to compliment him, and a whine slipped out instead. How pathetic was that?

"James really wants to climb up the Evil Tower," she said in a rush. "That's what he calls it. Mom's still too tired, so I should probably take him. Maybe Wednesday after school."

On Wednesdays the *collège* got out at noon, and the

little kids had no school at all.

"How about I come along, too?" asked Valko. "I've been under the tower about a million times, but I've never actually gone up."

Maya was still feeling slightly bad about James at the end of the day, so she spent five euros on a windup clown figure with a flashing nose that she had seen him admire in the toy store around the corner. Something about the packaging intrigued her, to tell the truth. One of those rounded plastic containers that resist your scissors to the death. She carved the toy clown out of its plastic casing very carefully and kept the shell.

And on Wednesday, Valko turned out to have been totally serious about the expedition to the Eiffel Tower.

"Check out my sturdy tower-climbing shoes!" he said, showing Maya his sneakers. Whether they were any different from the shoes he wore every other day, however, Maya couldn't have said.

James was practically floating with happiness and excitement when they picked him up at the apartment after school. Maya couldn't help but notice the relieved look on her mother's face, too. Looking forward to some quiet rest time, probably, while her kids were off climbing iron stairs: normal. The way any mother might feel. Right?

She looked again. It is one of the terrible things you start doing, when you get older and wiser: You can't help yourself; you look again.

Her mother was listening very intently to Valko at that moment, her cheek propped up on her thin, delicate hand. She must have just asked him a question, because her eyes had that interested flicker in them, very dark and alive in her too-pale face.

"So in some ways, I don't know what I am," Valko was saying, almost wistfully. "Half this and half that, by now. It's so bad I only dream in Bulgarian on, you know, odd-numbered days."

Then he laughed, and Maya's mother's eyes laughed, too, but that wasn't the terrible part. The terrible part was that even while he was laughing, Valko turned toward Maya, just for a second, and on his face were still etched all those things he hadn't yet had time enough to squirrel away properly: how surprised he was by what he couldn't help but have noticed about Maya's mother, how surprised he was and how sorry. *But, Maya, you never told me your mother was sick.* That's what his face said in that very short slice of time.

When your mother has been ill for a long, long time, your own eyes get used to it, the way callused hands have gotten used to their oars. You keep rowing on and on, and you don't look back, not too much: just the next patch of water, and the next, and the next. Until, that is, some kindhearted person comes into the room who hasn't been there all along, the way you have, and they look at her with their terrible uncallused eyes and say—actually, it doesn't matter what they say. Their eyes make your eyes see it all over again: the odd bruises lingering on the side of her paste-colored face; the still wispy, short hair; the beautiful, fragile, fading skin.

Maya dug her nails into her palm, to keep herself steady.

"Listen, now, you'd better get going," said Maya's mother, still smiling. "I think James may just pop with impatience if you don't head out soon."

The Davidsons' apartment was ridiculously close to the Eiffel Tower. You just walked down the rue de Grenelle three blocks, right past the lost children's melancholy little fountain, and there it was, looming up at the other end of a long green park. "Looming" was a word that turned up from time to time in books Maya had read, but she saw now that nothing on earth—not crises, shortages, dangers, icebergs—could possibly loom as convincingly as the Eiffel Tower, which grew larger and vaster with every step you took in its direction.

Before they crossed the last strip of road between them and the tower, they all three craned their heads far back and let their eyes climb up the curving lines way into the impossible air. It remade space all around them. Everything flat gained unexpected, astonishing depth. Maya's stomach began to feel just the slightest bit strange.

"Wow!" said James. "Wow! Wow! Wow! The Evil Tower! And NOW we get to go up to the very, very top!"

But the lines for the elevators were incredibly long; the snaking crowds waiting for their turn to buy tickets and zip up to the very, very top covered about a third of that enormous plaza between the tower's feet.

"Come on," said Valko. "Look how short the line for the stairs is. This way! We'll walk up."

"But I *like* elevators," said James a little sadly, as he trailed along after Valko. He cheered up once they were actually on the stairs, though. It was like climbing up inside the legs of a great machine. Climbing up and up and up, until beyond the metal lattice the world began to swim.

Once they had reached the second floor, Maya had to distract James from the sad news that tourists were not allowed to climb the stairs any higher, so she said he could take a couple of coins from her and try looking through one of the telescopes. It took him a long time to determine which telescope was the best one, but finally it was the glimpse of his very own school down below and to the east that decided him.

"I can see the trees in the courtyard!" he said. "That's where we play pirates and burglars during recess. . . . Don't wobble me, Maya! And look! There's the Salamander House! This is great!"

Maya looked down, her heart suddenly thudding away as if some secret of hers had been discovered. There it was, indeed: the Salamander House, right at the end of the short street far below where James's school was. That much she could see without the help of any telescope. James, his eye glued to the end of the telescope, suddenly began waving his hand in a merry arc.

"James! What are you doing?" said Maya.

"He's there again," said James. "The man in the window."

"Stop that!" said Maya. "Let me look."

She was not as gentle as she might have been, but the coins would run out in a minute, and fear was unexpectedly bubbling up in her chest.

"What man?" Valko asked James.

"He's interested in us," said James. "He has glasses like a spy! He talked to Daddy the first day, and when he saw us, he said we were perfect and charming. I think he's nice."

"Perfect and charming!" said Valko, half-teasing. "Are you sure about that?"

"That's *exactly* what he said, right, Maya? Didn't he say that, Maya? Maya!"

But Maya was trying to concentrate.

She had found the house right away, all its carvings and stone creatures crisply etched into the telescope's field of vision. Maya even thought she could see the door's bronze salamander, its head turned wonderingly in her direction. She moved the telescope a half inch higher, and there on his little balcony was the same dark-haired young man who had been standing there weeks ago, on that first morning in Paris. Who had come out of that door and walked right to their own apartment building and left a business card behind that said, "HENRI DE FOURCROY, DIRECTOR." The very same one. He had what looked like binoculars in his hands. Yes, definitely binoculars. He was looking through them toward the entrance of James's school; then in one fluid motion he turned the binoculars right up toward Maya and James and Valko. He was looking at them. He was totally looking at them.

She dropped the telescope as if it had stung her.

"Maya!" said James. "Give it back! It's my turn!"

"Not now," said Maya. "Money ran out. Come away from here."

"Was he there?" asked Valko. "Who is he?"

"Let's go back down," said Maya.

At least inside the ironwork of the tower's legs they would not be so visible, so terribly visible.

"Okay, okay," said Maya to Valko as they descended from step to step to step (and her words came out in a jumbled, jouncing rush). "I forgot to tell you about this part. He's the head of that Society thing, the one on the avenue Rapp. But his name is Fourcroy. Like the old guy with the sets: Remember I told you about him? So maybe this guy's even a relative or something, since the old one is. But the weird thing is, he paid for us to come to France.

I mean, the *Society* did. They gave my dad money—a fellowship. And the apartment, too."

She had to pause for a moment to catch her breath; that's how fast they were going down those stairs.

"Hunh," said Valko, shaking his head. "Are you saying the guy in charge of all the Beautiful People is maybe your relative? And he invited you to Paris?"

"He didn't say he was a relative," said Maya. "If he even is."

They were finally back out in the September sun, no longer filtered through wire safety fences and woven iron.

"That was six hundred steps!" said James. "I was counting almost all of the way. That was maybe more than six hundred steps!"

Maya heaved a sigh of relief, glad to be back on the ground—and less visible. But before she knew it, Valko and James had led her right back down the street past James's school, past the old lady always plonked on the bench at the corner, past the spindly tree where the crosswalk ended, and there, right in front of her now, was the salamander on the door again, turning his head right around as if he had a message for her. Something to say.

"Maya?" said Valko. "Are you all right?"

"It shouldn't be *moving* like that," said Maya in some distress. "Should it?"

"Maya?"

"The salamander!" she said. "You really don't see it?"

"It's metal," said Valko, in his sensible way. "I think you'd need a blowtorch to budge it."

"Oh, come *on*," said Maya, grabbing James's hand to pull them all farther down the street to the right, away from the door and the salamander and that building with all its flowing waves of stone.

But at that very second (Maya and Valko flattened themselves as inconspicuously as possible against the wall), the door of the Salamander House flew open, and a woman stepped through it. She was very beautiful and very young, and her clothes were far too fancy for three o'clock on a Wednesday afternoon. Really, she looked like someone who belonged in a magazine, not on an actual sidewalk. (Even a sidewalk in Paris.) But what was most striking about her was that she was happy, happy, happy, quite glowing with happiness and relief.

"Oh, he has saved my life," she was saying to the man coming through the door behind her. "Can't you feel it? He and the *anbar*. . . ."

"Come, *chérie*," said the man. "It is a feast to look on you."

And it really was. You wanted to stare and stare. Or maybe even go up to her and say just anything, in the odd chance she would turn her radiant eyes right on you. And the man was glowing, too. Maya had never seen anything quite like it. But Valko poked her sharply in the arm, and she pulled her eyes away from them, so as not to be caught staring.

The couple turned the other way, heading up the street past the old lady on her bench, and Maya had just given James's hand a brisk tug, as a way of reminding him they were actually on their way home, when a low whistle made her look back toward the door of the Salamander House, where Valko was standing, quite casual-like, his left leg angled in a slightly awkward way.

He had caught the outer door with his foot before it could close.

"Well, hey," he said, his voice almost a shadow of itself. "Look at this."

And he slipped right in through the salamander door—and held it open after him.

7

THE PURPLE-EYED FOURCROY

Maya had an impression of elaborately carved walls and stairs twining away from the hall and light spilling in from the courtyard ahead, but those first few seconds she was whispering so fiercely at Valko that nothing else was quite in focus.

"What are you doing!" she was saying. "We can't just wander in like this!"

But of course by then she already had, and, what's more, had brought James right in through the door with her. He was straining now to reach the wildly complicated metal railings that slithered up around pairs of marble pillars on either side of the entryway.

"Look! It's squids!" said James.

Well, true, there might be something aquatic going on in those patterns of coiled iron, but Maya had other things on her mind at the moment.

"Shh," she said, and tightened her grip on his hand

another notch or two. "Come on, Valko, let's go."

"You know who those people outside were?" said Valko, scanning the walls and doorways with his bright gray eyes. "The Dolphin's parents."

"You're kidding," said Maya. They hadn't looked very much like parents to her, so young and so radiant. It twisted something sharp in her, thinking how old and tired her mother would look placed next to that beautiful woman stepping across the threshold with such confidence and grace. "They can't be old enough to have a kid our age. Can they?"

"They're rich," said Valko, as if that explained it all. "Hey, and look at this: There he is, your possible Uncle Fourcroy."

By the inner door there was a panel with names and buzzers.

She pulled James up the two marble steps to the door to see for herself. And there it was: *Henri de Fourcroy*. In tiny handwriting that looked about a million years old. He hadn't been in the phone book, but here he was all the same.

"Can I push the button?" asked James.

"No!" said Maya.

"Not even if he's really truly our uncle?" said James.

And at that moment a voice on the intercom cleared its throat. It sounded almost amused.

"Dear children," it said, in a very French sort of English. "If you have come here for visiting me, then you should certainly continue up the stairs on the right, should you not? Fourth floor."

"*You pressed that button!*" said Maya under her breath to James. His eyes were wide. He gave his head a shake, staring all the time at the panel on the wall that had so unexpectedly begun to speak.

"I did not!" he said, using his ordinary voice, the voice that carried so well on playgrounds, in classrooms, and on public buses.

"Excuse us," said Valko into the intercom in his best French, which was still significantly better than Maya's best French. "Excuse us for disturbing you, *monsieur*."

"But you aren't disturbing me at all!" said the voice. "And if I am your uncle, then we should definitely converse, is that not so? I am unlatching the door now: here."

And there was a click from the double glass doors ahead of them as the latch was released. Valko caught the door with his hand and then looked back at Maya with a questioning shrug. And she—

What could she say in her defense? The voice speaking to them over the intercom, like the elegant young man she knew it belonged to, had a certain magnetic allure. Indeed, it was one of the pleasantest, most appealing voices Maya had ever heard: at once friendly and welcoming and warm. It was a voice that inspired confidence, even trust. And there had been a salamander on the Cabinet of Earths: Yes, she was curious about all the salamanders. That was probably part of it, too.

"Be good children," said the voice as an afterthought, "and bring up my mail, if you would. On the table in the vestibule. *Merci bien!*"

The stairwell was beautiful, too; more loops and tendrils in the stained-glass windows bringing light into the stairway from the courtyard in back.

Maya clutched Monsieur de Fourcroy's packet of letters in one hand and James's warm palm in the other. She was surprising herself, by walking so bravely up these stairs, and she wasn't sure yet whether she liked that feeling.

"Your *Uncle Fourcroy*!" said Valko, more than once, as they climbed the stairs. And he shook his head in disbelief.

Maya tried to shut him up with a glare, but the stairs were a bit too shadowy for glares.

"Remember to be very polite," she said to James. "He's not really our uncle. Some kind of very, very distant cousin, maybe. So just be polite."

But when they got to the landing of the fourth floor and the dark wooden door swung open before them, James stuck out his free hand as if there were no doubt about any of it at all.

"*Bonjour*, Uncle-Cousin!"

And the brown-haired man who had opened the door laughed aloud and shook James's hand with mock seriousness.

"But I haven't met you all," he said. "Not all of you, I don't believe."

"I'm James Davidson," said James. "You sort of met me and Maya the first day we were in Paris. Right? Remember that?"

"And I'm Valko," said Valko.

Maya was having a difficult time speaking just then, because in the light that spilled onto the landing, she had just caught a glimpse of Henri de Fourcroy's incredible eyes, which were not just blue, but purple, the purple of the tall irises that sprang up every spring under the liquidambar trees back home in California, the purple of grape juice, of felt pens, of make-believe jewels.

Once when her mother had taken her for a haircut, Maya had been paging through the glossy magazines in the waiting room and had come across a page filled with pictures of extraordinary eyes: blue-green, green-blue, violet, orange—incredible things! It turned out that if you wore contact lenses, you could have eyes any color you wanted, almost. Even pink or gold! Polka dots! And for one heady moment, Maya had dreamed of arriving at school with brilliant turquoise eyes, of being a different sort of Maya entirely, dazzling and mysterious. And then she had put that magazine down and forgotten all about it until now.

The eyes of the elegant young man at the door were exactly the sort of astonishing purple-violet-blue that people might pay money to wear, but Maya was absolutely sure they were real.

So that's why he had to wear those glasses, she thought. Because passersby might stop and stare.

"The scientist's children!" said the man, and he stood back to let them through. "Of course! And now you say we are cousins? Well, what a surprise! How lovely to see you again! Come in!"

"Actually, I'm just a friend," said Valko as he stepped over the threshold.

"Come in anyway," said the man, and then he turned his purple eyes right on Maya and smiled slightly.

"How kind of you to come," he said.

Maya handed him his letters without saying a word, and his eyes rested on her thoughtfully for a moment, almost as if he were seeing something in her she knew nothing about. And then he was focused again on James, who was, as usual, being delightful.

"Come sit down and explain yourselves," said the purple-eyed man. Off the end of the long hall was a living room, with comfortable chairs and a fireplace. "There are little candies somewhere here. Ah, there they are. They have caramel in them, do you mind?"

James did not mind at all!

"Ask your sister to tell me why you count as cousins," said the man to James in a playful sort of way, after everyone except Maya had eaten a couple of caramels.

"Tell him, Maya," said James, turning for a moment to smile at her while his hand darted out for another sweet. "He's our uncle, right?"

"I'm sorry," said Maya, her voice sounding to her as if it had stayed at the other end of the long hall. "We shouldn't be bothering you this way. I mean, we're probably not related at all. It was just the family tree—those Fourcroys."

"A family tree with Fourcroys in it!" exclaimed the elegant young man with a smile. "But, you know, Fourcroys are very rare! I am practically the only one left, I do believe."

"Except for the old man," said James, confidingly. "Right?"

The purple eyes became very quick and sharp, for all that the face they were in held on to its warm and welcoming smile.

"What old man do you mean, Cousin?" said the elegant young man, and he flicked his eyes from James to Maya and back to James.

The one who takes no more deliveries from you!

But of course she couldn't say that. Indeed, she couldn't say much, not out loud. Her mouth wouldn't quite open, or it would open and the sound wouldn't come. She had wanted to ask all sorts of questions, about the Society he supposedly ran, about the bronze salamander downstairs that kept forgetting it should not be alive, about the old man with his opera sets and his Cabinet of Earths, but the words would not form themselves. Something wouldn't let her speak, not about any of that, not in this place.

It was a strange feeling, and she didn't like it very much. Especially with everybody turning to look at her, and her mouth opening and closing like a flustered fish.

"Maya, are you all right?" said Valko.

"A little dizzy, maybe," said Maya. And alarmed. But she didn't want to admit to that for some reason, not here.

"There's a washroom near the door you came in by," said the man kindly. "Why don't you go and splash your face?"

So that's what she did. It was all right to leave James for a moment, because Valko was right there. James would chatter, but Valko would watch out for him. And she did feel strange.

Maya walked back down the hall to the bathroom and splashed her face with cool water. It brought her back to herself, more or less. She found she was curious again. The layout of the apartment, for instance: That was strange. It seemed to stretch around the courtyard like an angular doughnut, because here was a hall heading away from the street, and she was sure there had been yet another hall peeking out from the door at the back of the living room. Through the doorways on the left came light from the street windows. She glanced into a couple of those rooms on her way back. Studies of some kind. A sweet smell. The second study had a great, old desk in the center of it, and on that desk there stood the strangest apparatus. She slipped through the door for a moment to take a closer look. The sweetness was stronger in here, not just sweet, but musky-sweet. A lovely smell.

There was a dark little bowl on the desk, with a candle burning in it. And suspended over the candle fire was another, smaller bowl, and in it, melting, was something translucent and gold, like honey, but harder than honey. And fragrant! From that slowly melting cake of gold, not two inches in diameter, came the heady, wonderful sweetness that filled the air of this room and had called her in. She was so lost in that perfume that when a bell suddenly rang—the door! it must be the front door!—she jumped and looked around herself in panic. She hadn't meant to sneak about like this, poking and prying. And now he would catch her at it! How awful.

Her uncle-cousin's footsteps went striding down the hall past the room where Maya found herself hiding.

A woman's voice at the door, a pleading voice. Maya couldn't make out all the words. Just *anbar.* That strange word again. *Anbar,* and something else that Maya couldn't hear. That she was sick—was that it? And her uncle-cousin was replying in his patient, pleasant way, perhaps saying that he was busy, perhaps telling her to come back some other time.

She considered hiding under the desk. No, that was ridiculous. And then she looked around the room again and noticed—the complexity of the wood paneling had tricked her eyes at first—that the room had another door, after all. Past the desk with its purring candle and the mysterious cake melting into some kind of slow honey was a door with a handle. Beside it, a little table with what must be two more of those cakes, only these were in tidy little red velvet cases. Looking like something familiar, like—but the noun slipped away when she groped for it.

She put her left hand on the doorknob. And as the door began to open, her right hand, without any warning at all, reached over to the little red cases of incense, or whatever it was, and whisked one deep into the pocket of her coat. She was through the door by the time her mind caught up with her hand, and then she had only time enough to catch her breath in surprise and close the door quietly behind her, because she was back in the living room at the end of the hall, and Valko and James had turned in their chairs to look over at her, and the footsteps of her uncle-cousin were already coming back in this direction down the hall.

"Oh, good, you're back!" said James when he saw her. "What took you so long? We're going to get our pictures taken!"

Indeed, the purple-eyed Fourcroy was now coming back through the door with the strangest old camera in his hands, like nothing Maya had ever seen, all bulbous with attachments and lenses and impossibly complicated meters.

"Are you recovered, little cousin-or-niece?" he asked Maya with great courtesy.

"Yes, yes," said Maya. "I'm fine."

But in fact she was restless. Itching to leave. The purple-eyed Fourcroy took no notice.

"We've agreed, James and I, that such a reunion of cousins, since it seems we may be cousins, should be documented. Do you mind? Hold steady, now."

And he took a photograph right then and there, with Maya still half turned toward James's chair and Valko looking over in her direction as if he had something in particular to say. Some hidden machinery in the camera popped and whirred. The elegant young man set it down very carefully on the table and smiled.

"So!" he said.

"I've never seen a camera like *that*," said James. "Wow!"

"Very old," said the elegant young man. "An absolute antique. Have another caramel, won't you?"

Valko was craning his neck to get a better look at the camera, too, but the purple-eyed Fourcroy kept getting in his way with that dish of candies.

"We *have* to go home now," said Maya. "James! Let's go."

"Thank you for coming to see your old cousin Fourcroy," said the man, in his friendly way, and he smiled as he said it, since he was so very much the opposite of old.

"Thank you for the candy," said James, and Maya and Valko echoed something similar.

"I didn't *quite* finish all of mine," added James.

"Well, then, you'll have to come back," said the cousin-uncle. "And have more sweets another day. If I give you the entrance code, it will be easier for you to come visit, won't it? 1901."

"Come on, James," said Maya. "You can't take more candy now!"

"It's quite an easy code to remember," continued the cousin-uncle. "It's the year the house was built, you see."

"That's very long ago," said James.

Their cousin-uncle looked at James, and for a moment there was a flicker of feeling in his extraordinary eyes that Maya could not make sense of—amusement or pain or some odd mixture of the two.

"Perhaps it is," he said. "What long lives they have, buildings!"

As they spiraled back down the stairs to the ground, Maya remembered what it was the little honey cakes reminded her of: *rosin*. That's what violinists put on their bows to get more sound out of their strings—was it made out of tree sap? Something like that.

Maya's mother used to play the violin, back before she got so sick. Then one day, she said the violin was too heavy, and her arm was too puffy, and her fingers too stiff, and she had closed up the rosin in its little satin bag and put the bow away and shut the violin case to wait until she was "really healthy again."

And when was that going to be? Not just not sick, but her own wonderful self again, through and through. That was what Maya most urgently wanted to know. She emerged into the sunlight of the avenue Rapp, with James and Valko chattering at her about uncles, candies, and doors—and her heart caught her completely by surprise by being all tangled up in that other, deepest question:

When, oh when, cried her heart, *was her mother finally going to be well?*

8

WORRYING

Every single person on the planet probably has some bad habit they'd rather the rest of us didn't know about. People leave their underwear on the floor or wash their hands too much or write love letters to television stars or always put off doing their math until the last minute. Maya, for instance, was a worrier. She knew she was, but it was still aggravating when her mother pointed it out ("You worry too much, honey-bun! It'll all be okay, really it will"—though the universe didn't have a very good track record on these things, as far as Maya could tell). As long as she could remember, Maya had always worried with her hands as well as her mind: She would pick at loose threads on her clothes until the edges unraveled, trouble her fingernails down to the quick, roll the wax that slipped down the candlesticks into smooth and milky pills. And scabs! They didn't stand a chance.

"You have very busy fingers," her mother had said one

day, half-alarmed and half-amused. What had Maya been worrying away at then? It was long ago. Maybe the hair of one of her dolls. But what Maya most remembered about that moment was the odd feeling of pride that had rippled through her. *Busy fingers*—and they were all hers, to put to work on whatever she wanted. They just needed something to do.

When she got a bit older, she had found that the right sort of project (if it was fussy enough and complicated) could satisfy her hands almost as much as picking and pulling and worrying at things. So that very evening, after James had finished chattering about towers and uncles and gone yawning to bed, Maya got out some scissors and glue, little screwdrivers and thread, whatever she could find, and let her busy fingers make what it was they were moved to make, just to keep them out of trouble, while her mind worked away at its own rough places.

(Why was her mother still so tired?) Rummaging through the big supply closet in the study, she found some tiny plastic bottle tops that could serve as glasses.

(Her father saw it, too; that look on his face at breakfast!) And glue that when shaped into sticky little white peas could be dipped in cardamom or cinnamon and made into blobs of miniature sand.

(If her mother was sick again, would they tell her?) Rectangles of plastic became the shelves; she built the

cabinet's frame from tiny dowels, glue, and clay.

(*They would try to hide it from her, probably, as long as they could.*) It was the oddly familiar curve of that plastic casing that had done it, the shell from which she had extracted James's silly windup clown. That had probably given her the idea.

(*She would watch them like a hawk; she would not let them fool her into thinking all was fine.*) More glue to fit the shelves with their rows of tiny glasses into the frame with its rounded front. And then there was just the question of the salamander.

"Maya, hon?" Her mother stuck her head around the door. "Are you really still up? You'll be misery itself tomorrow, if you don't get some sleep. What's that you're working on?"

But Maya had already swept the little cabinet behind her and under the bed. It was a private thing. Nobody should see it. It needed her. It was hers to protect, hers to keep safe.

And she absolutely could not talk about it. Not at all. When Maya and Valko talked about Cousin Louise, or the various Fourcroys, Maya would get stuck, sometimes, if the topic got too close to the Cabinet, which was too private for words. Sometimes she would open her mouth and then find there was nothing she was able to say. Her jaw would just stick for a bit, while her brain tried to find a way around the topic. It was a little unsettling, to tell the truth. It was odd. But then, odd things seemed to be going on all around her these days.

A day after their unexpected visit to the Salamander House, for instance, Valko and Maya were chatting in the courtyard at school, and the Dolphin and his elegant gang were hanging out, looking lovely and bored, by the classroom steps. Pretty much like every other morning recess. And then the wind changed. (Literally: Maya had to brush the hair back out of her eyes.) And for some reason, when the breeze got as far as the Dolphin's crowd, a few of them turned their heads and looked over at Maya and Valko, almost as if they thought the wind had been conjured up by someone on purpose. This was strange, because never yet in the first month of classes had the Dolphin or any of his well-dressed friends ever so much as glanced in Maya's direction. And now they were looking her way with what might even be actual interest. In fact, a couple of them almost seemed to be sniffing the air as if they had just caught the scent of something they rather liked.

Maya and Valko looked at each other, and Valko, who had some nimble muscles in his face, raised a questioning eyebrow.

"Okay, that's weird," he said to Maya. "Did one of us just make a really loud noise or something?"

"One of them's coming over," said Maya. "Oh boy, the Dolphin himself. And what's her name, that really blond girl."

"Cécile," said Valko. "Wonder what they want."

Well, they didn't want Valko, apparently. The Dolphin and Cécile sailed up to the two of them but did not so much as glance in Valko's direction. The Dolphin just passed a lazy hand over the top of his burnished hair and gave Maya an assessing sort of smile, the slightest bit vague around the edges.

"You're the new girl, I think," he said. And then he sniffed the air again. "From the United States."

"Hello," said Maya.

"How do you like Paris?" said Cécile, coming up behind him.

"It's beautiful," said Maya, a bit distracted by the sarcastic waves she could feel flowing in her direction from Valko.

The Dolphin and Cécile stood there for a moment, looking at her, and then Cécile pulled out a printed card from her bag and handed it over in one smooth, graceful motion, almost as if her hands had nothing to do with the rest of her, and then the two of them drifted back to the rest of their people.

Maya gave herself a little shake, like a rabbit once the fox has faded back into the woods.

"Did you hear all that snuffling?" said Valko. "I have a cold, and I'm quieter than that. I mean, what was *that* all about?"

"No idea," said Maya, and then she looked down at the card in her hands. "I'm invited to something. A party. In October. Weird."

The bell was ringing already, so she stuffed the invitation into her notebook and shrugged. It wasn't as if her name were actually written on the card; it must have been a whim that had come over them, the Dolphin and Cécile. Those pretty faces, sniffing the air as if it carried some trace of her. She didn't like that at all. It was beyond weird, when you thought about it. It was out-and-out creepy.

Then a couple of days later Maya put her hand deep into her coat pocket, looking for change, and found the little round container of *anbar* still hiding there. As soon as she touched it, the memory came flooding back, of the moment when her hand had just shot right out and plucked the case off the young Fourcroy's table. Now the pretty box of *anbar* seemed to burn her fingers. She was so surprised to find it in her hand, in fact, that she dropped it right onto the floor and then had to stoop very fast to pick it up before her mother could come back into the hall and start asking questions.

She had never stolen anything before. It didn't seem

like the sort of thing she would do. And yet somehow she had done it! The fragrant little box almost winked at her as she hid it behind the books on her bedroom shelf. *What else was she capable of?* she wondered.

The Dolphin's crowd no longer sniffed the air, the next day, when Maya stood in the school yard. Whatever aura she had held for them for those few days seemed to have evaporated into thin air. Odd, though, all the same.

Her mother was fighting off a touch of the flu. That's what her father said the morning her mother didn't even get out of bed to see James and Maya off to school. Maya's fingers itched with worry. She actually had to go back into her bedroom for a moment and run her hands lightly over the little cabinet she was making—the salamander was very good now; she had used some of James's modeling clay, and the tiny head turned at just the right quizzical angle—before she could face breakfast and school.

"Don't fret about it," said her father, though there was a little crease of trouble on his forehead. "I'm taking the day off from the lab. She'll be drowning in chicken broth and attention."

Maya could hardly look at him, because otherwise she knew the knot of worry in her might just fly out all over the place, and then what would they do? James had to be gotten cheerfully to school. That's the way they ran things on days like this, Maya and her father. Still, it was like finding the same old load of bricks on your shoulders again, the weight you thought you had finally shed.

But when she climbed the stairs at the end of the day (a few minutes later than usual, because there were math problems to copy out from Valko's notebook), Maya caught the scent of something encouraging: the faint aroma of baking. Half a flight later she knew the baking must be happening in her own apartment, because the smell had evolved into something more specific: chocolate chip cookies, and the Davidsons were the only family in the building that ever baked something as American as chocolate chip cookies. More specifically, only Maya's mother ever baked them. Maya's feet fairly danced up the last dozen steps to the door. Everything must be all right, if her mother was baking again.

But it was the inexpressive back of Cousin Louise she found bent over a tray of cookies when Maya came sailing through the apartment door. James was standing there, too, a toothpick in one solemn hand.

"We're seeing if they're done," he said to Maya.

"But where's Mom?"

"Mom got the recipe out, but then she had to go to the hospital," said James.

"What?" said Maya. "What?"

"Maya, *bonjour,*" said Cousin Louise, turning to look at Maya with her bland eyes. "You are not to worry, says your father. The hospital is just a precaution. And James wanted very much to continue with the cookies, though I am not really qualified."

"We're making cookies for that uncle," said James. "In the Salamander House."

"What?" said Maya again. Her school backpack clonked heavily to the floor.

"Because we ate his candy up," said James. "Remember how we went to see him and ate all his dessert up? I told Mom about that, and she said we should bake him something. And so we were going to do it today, and then she had to go for a checkup."

"A checkup?" said Maya. The happiness had drained out of her so abruptly that she felt a little dazed.

"At the doctor's," said James, and he poked another cookie with his toothpick.

"You don't have to test cookies like that," said Maya, distracted. "If they look done, they're done."

"Cousin Louise said perhaps we should be extra careful."

"It's that I know nothing about cookies," said Cousin Louise in French. "Now that you are here, Maya, we can go to this other Fourcroy you have found."

"But what is wrong with Mom?" said Maya.

Cousin Louise and James both turned away from the cookies to look at Maya. Cousin Louise's expression was unreadable, but James looked startled.

"It's a checkup, right?" he said. "Like when you get the plastic dinosaur from the treasure chest afterward. Only I don't think they give dinosaurs to grown-ups."

"Your father said not to worry," said Cousin Louise.

Maya had to go out into the hall for a moment to bite back a lot of loud shouting words. Not worry! Maybe that worked on little kids like James. Maybe if you spent your life being almost invisible, like Cousin Louise, you eventually weren't able to tell the difference anymore between empty words and the truth. When she was finally able to come back in, Cousin Louise and James were already putting the cookies into a tin.

"Time for us to go," said Cousin Louise. "We have worked it out, James and I. I am not going to do any talking."

"She's our nanny," said James, looking smug. "Our *nounou*." A lot of the kids in his class were picked up by nannies at the end of the day.

"What I want is to look, quietly," said Cousin Louise.

Maya felt tired already. They were really planning to take cookies to the purple-eyed Fourcroy in the Salamander House? All right, then; why not.

James carried the tin of cookies; Maya sagged along

behind, worrying about their mother. And Cousin Louise walked in their shadow, and her thoughts, if she had any, were inscrutable.

At the entrance to the Salamander House, however, Maya felt a papery hand tighten itself around her arm.

"Familiar," said Cousin Louise. She was looking up at the door, the building, the carvings crawling everywhere. "Look at her, for instance!"

It was the young woman whose head looked out over the street from the top of the door. The expression on her stone face was sad and wise, somehow; she hardly seemed to notice the fox draped around her neck.

"It's a Maya statue," said James proudly. "See?"

"Strange," said Cousin Louise in a thoughtful voice. "*Et là*, the little salamander on the door. I have seen it before, I think."

Maya opened her mouth to point out that a similar salamander had looked out at them from the frame of the Cabinet of Earths, but the words refused to be spoken out loud. She had to close her mouth with the faintest little pop, like the noise a fish makes when it smacks its lips underwater. So instead she stepped up to the sill and typed in the code for the door: 1901.

"What if he's not home?" said James. "Will we leave the cookies here anyway, if the uncle-cousin's not home?"

The door opened with a little click. James slipped

under Maya's arm and into the hallway beyond, but Cousin Louise stayed still for a moment longer, looking up at the building and thinking something over. Her vague, inexpressive eyes seemed almost—but perhaps it was just a trick of the light—clouded with doubt.

"Are you coming in?" said Maya, as politely as she could manage. She could already hear James looking noisily for the right button on the intercom inside. "F!" James was saying. "F! Like Forest!"

"Caution," said Cousin Louise under her breath. "Caution."

But she came in all the same.

9

HOT CHOCOLATE AND *ANBAR*

They tiptoed up the stairs to the fourth floor and right into an argument.

"Be reasonable," a man was saying to the purple-eyed Fourcroy. "You know she can't go on without it. She feels like she's dying, she says. Only the *anbar* really perks her up anymore. It is the only miracle she has left, now that time looms so very large before her."

Henri de Fourcroy looked slightly bored. His eyes wandered away from the man at his door and caught sight of James and Maya coming up the stairs, Cousin Louise trudging along behind them.

"Ah, but *monsieur*!" he said, his beautiful eyes brightening. "As you can see, my guests have arrived! Perhaps another day?"

And then he managed in one flowing gesture to usher James and Maya (and Cousin Louise behind them) into his entrance hall—and leave the complaining man outside on the landing behind the door.

"We brought you cookies," said James, holding the tin out in front of him. "We baked them ourselves."

"How kind of you," said their cousin-uncle. "How unnecessarily thoughtful!"

Maya was feeling rather unsettled, for some reason, and Cousin Louise lowered herself into a chair by the door.

"That's our babysitter today," said James, leaning toward the cousin-uncle in a confiding sort of way. "Our mother would have come, but she's sick."

The purple-eyed Fourcroy clicked his tongue against his palate in a sympathetic way.

"Come on in, come on in," he said, and he led them down the hall to the living room.

Cousin Louise just stayed where she was, a human-sized shadow in a chair, but the younger Fourcroy took no notice of her. He was quite engrossed in his conversation with James, and Maya walked down the hall silently behind the two of them, her eyes, for the most part, on the floor. If she looked left, she might see the study again, the one where her hand had snatched the small velvet case and made her a thief. She tried instead not to look in any particular direction at all. And then she heard James say, in his cheerful way—

"Hey, Uncle Fourcroy, what is *anbar*, anyway?"

"Shall we try these cookies of yours?" asked the cousin-uncle. "Should I pass around little plates? What do you think?"

"You don't need plates for chocolate chip cookies," said James. "You just reach in and pick them up, like this."

The carpet in this room was a deep red, with branches of green snaking through it and butterflies perched on the fuzzy woven twigs. And here and there in the pattern and branches and leaves, just the slightest hint—glinty silk eyes or flickery tail—of a salamander. Maya worked away at the wings of one of the bright little knotted butterflies with the toe of her shoe. It was a way of not listening too hard to the conversation James and the younger Fourcroy were having, and she became so engrossed in that carpet and those butterflies that she didn't even notice, for some time, that the conversation in the room had lulled, and Henri de Fourcroy was now looking straight at her.

"Will you also have a cookie, Maya?" asked the cousin-uncle.

She jumped in her chair.

"Yes, yes," she said. "Thank you."

"They are truly delicious," said the elegant young man with warmth. "I seem most fortunate in my choice of cousins."

"You were going to tell me what *anbar* is," said James.

Maya hushed him, but it made no difference. Henri de Fourcroy looked at James, and then (a moment later, perhaps?) relaxed into a broad smile.

"Have you heard of 'ambrosia'?" he said. "The food of the gods. Perhaps like these sweet cookies you have been so kind to bring?"

"*Anbar* is chocolate chip cookies?" said James.

"Well," said the purple-eyed Fourcroy. "A metaphysical substance, actually. Strange words, yes? But we use them to say that some things, dear James, cannot be made or explained by science alone. Many very useful and wonderful things! You could fill a whole pharmacy with them. That is, in fact, the chief work of our Society. Quite a noble and interesting work, too, if I do say so myself."

"You mean it's a *medicine*?" said James, sounding very disappointed.

"Much better than medicine," said the elegant young man. "Ambrosia from *a-mbrotos*, you know. A food for immortals. That's Greek, my young cousin. An old, old language. Could you stay a bit longer, so that I could prepare for you a little drink of *chocolat chaud*? Because that also, to be honest, may be a bit like ambrosia."

"Cocoa?" said James. "Maya, can we stay for cocoa? I really, really want to."

"And a little something special, perhaps," added the purple-eyed Fourcroy, with a smile, "for your sister, who seems like someone who might already appreciate the charms, as it were, of a thing like ambrosia. . . ."

"Let me go ask," said Maya, standing up right away. How eager she was to get out of this room and away from the discussion of *anbar*, *anbar*, *anbar*! Was that what he was getting at, with those hints and wise smiles? Had he guessed? Did he know? Oh, she hadn't meant to steal that little case; it had just happened. But here, in this place, she found herself feeling more and more uncomfortable.

The purple-eyed Fourcroy hardly noticed her; he was intent instead (as people usually were) on James, who was really on a roll today, all sweetness and charm. "Never much need to worry about James," her mother had said with a laugh once, when he had wandered off in the supermarket for a moment, only to reappear in the midst of a small crowd of doting clerks and checkers. "Everyone will always want to see him safely home!"

Oh, but thinking of her mother made Maya's stomach hurt. Was she all right? Were they back from the hospital, perhaps, by now?

In her worry she didn't even notice for a second or two that Cousin Louise's chair in the entry hall was empty. But she would never have just left them there! No, there she was, a shadowy figure signaling to Maya from the shadowy corridor that ran back into the darkness to the left.

Maya went down that other hall to the doorway where

Cousin Louise now stood.

"Do you see this?" asked Cousin Louise, in a voice so quiet it was almost drowned out by the ticking of a clock farther down the hall.

Maya looked through the door. It was a room that looked out on the inner courtyard. The walls were green. And in that room was (Maya's mind faltered for a moment, trying to find a word that described what she was seeing) a chair.

A dentist's chair. No. A dentist's chair if that dentist lived in some other, more ancient universe than ours. Everywhere vines and branches of metal twining about. A bright phoenix with amber eyes flying up one of the sides. Were those candlesticks along the top?

And arranged in neat rows on the old-fashioned counter on the left side of the room: tongs and test tubes, spoons and funnels, odd twisting devices she had never even imagined in her strangest nightmares, all embellished and bright, all alive with patterns, all beautiful, all full of loveliness and menace.

"Oh!" said Maya, and the dry weight of Cousin Louise's hand settled in warning on her arm.

That was not all: from the ceiling hung a long loop of string. And from the loop dangled (like a small, square sheet hung up to dry) a photograph. Not an ordinary photograph, but something all shivering with light and depth. She shook off Cousin Louise's arm and went forward a couple of steps, just to see (but some part of her seemed already to know what she would find, and that part trembled and shrank back).

A shining, luminous boy. And next to him two shadowy figures, the outline of one of them slightly marred, in the place where that person's coat pocket must have been, by one pinprick of white light, as though something had pierced the picture at some point and flawed it, when it was being developed.

"Time for us to go," said Cousin Louise. "Quiet, quiet. Go back to fetch your brother, please, and we will leave."

James! But that's who it was, the luminous boy. It was James.

And there was writing along the bottom edge of the photograph, she saw that now: "*Charismatograph reading: 326.8_X. A record!—and they are Lavirottes.*"

And in smaller letters still: "*Perfect arrangement. The Cab. needs its new Keeper.*"

"Maya," said Cousin Louise from the doorway. "Touch nothing. We must immediately leave."

Maya jumped a little in her skin. Then she turned around and walked back to the entry hall, back down the other corridor to the comfortable room where she could hear the clear voice of her brother, laughing.

"There you are! Can we?" he said as soon as he saw

her. "Can we stay for cocoa?"

Henri de Fourcroy looked up at Maya, his purple-blue eyes again seeming to take the measure of something in her.

"We have to go now," said Maya, keeping her voice as steady as possible. She could not quite bring herself to look into those lovely, unsettling eyes, so she directed everything she said to James alone. "Mom might be waiting for us, you know. She might be home already."

"But I'm glad you liked the cookies!" said James to the purple-eyed Fourcroy as Maya propelled him down the hall toward the door.

"Oh, very much!" said the cousin-uncle, and for a moment he looked as if he were remembering the flavor of something, and wanting more of it. Hungry. That was how he looked.

Cousin Louise stood up from her chair by the front door with all the convincing dullness of someone who had been sitting there for an hour without moving. You would really never guess, to look at her, that she was capable of poking about in an apartment's dark corners.

"Come, children," she said, and so they left, James waving good-bye as they started down the stairs.

Until they were back on the street and walking away from the salamander, neither Maya nor Cousin Louise said a word. James chattered on undaunted, and when they came to the next long block, Maya let go of his hand so he could skip ahead. She had been holding on to him too tightly: she had to shake her fingers to loosen them up again. But James bounced in zigzags along the broad sidewalk before them as if he hadn't noticed a thing.

"I was in that chair," said Cousin Louise out of the blue. "I remember that now. I was a tiny child in that chair. Only that. And his eyes."

"Not *his* eyes," said Maya. "He's too young."

"No, I am sure he is the one," said Cousin Louise in her flat voice. "Oh, what an unlucky family we are! He took me in. He's the one, without a doubt."

That couldn't be, of course. The purple-eyed Fourcroy was much younger than Cousin Louise, for one thing. But it seemed useless to point that out. Cousin Louise marched along the sidewalk, and Maya walked beside her, not daring to interrupt.

"And then I was different," said Cousin Louise. "After that, I was changed. It was him, I am completely certain. Ah, here we are."

James still had enough energy to run up the stairs, but nobody came striding to the apartment door when he rang and rang the bell. Maya, fifteen steps behind him, listened with every fiber of her being for her mother's footsteps, and heard nothing. No one was home, after all. The apartment seemed very dark and cold and strange, even after Cousin Louise had made her methodical way from room to room, turning on lights and taking eggs out of the refrigerator for an omelette.

They were eating that omelette (and listening to James talk about his plans for some game he was going to play with the other boys during tomorrow's morning recess), when there was finally the sound of a key in the door. Maya bolted into the hall: Her father was there, alone, pulling his jacket off, looking tired. She had gotten to him so quickly that she had caught a glimpse of his face before he had had time to put the proper parental expression on it (calm, comforting, confident). She had seen the familiar wear and worry there, the shadows under his cheekbones, before he brushed those shadows away and turned to greet her and James with a hug and a smile.

"She'll be fine," he said. "They're just keeping her overnight for observation."

"Observation?" said Maya.

"Oh, you know, running a few tests."

Tests. Maya was still digesting that word when Cousin Louise came rustling up behind them, reaching for her coat.

"And so I depart," she said. "Sylvie will be home tomorrow, I hope?"

Maya's father nodded. He was never quite comfortable around Cousin Louise. He became stiff, somehow, and he was not usually a stiff person.

But as Cousin Louise slipped out through the door, she put one cool hand on Maya's cheek and said, "Be careful, Maya. Be *prudente*."

Once Cousin Louise had gone, it turned out their father was too distracted to ask them anything about their afternoon. He just listened to James ramble on about the chocolate chip cookies and let the rest of it drop, to Maya's relief. They were all tired.

Before going to sleep that night, however, she brought out the envelope of old photographs again, all those shining children smiling up at her from under their long-ago caps and berets. They were special, she could see that. Special, like James was special. The camera had figured that out somehow; it had known enough to make Maya a dull shadow, too. But what they meant, those pictures, what they were *for*, exactly—that she couldn't understand.

(*The Cab. needs its new Keeper.* That's what the terrible photograph had said.)

Her fingers ran over the numbers on the back of the photographs, and the worry grew in her until she had to put the pictures away and instead bring out the little cabinet from its hiding spot. Just seeing it again made a difference, and then the simple work of touching up the miniature cabinet's salamander and phoenix with the bronze paint she had found in a shop around the corner settled her down and dulled the edges of her troubles: the shimmering photographs, the hospital room too far away where her mother was sleeping. The little cabinet glittered in the light of her bedroom lamp; it alone, of everything and everybody in Maya's world (with the usual exception of James), seemed content with the way things were going in the universe at the moment.

She put it on her table to let the paint dry, and even with her lamp turned off, the small cabinet continued to catch the tiny scraps of light that filtered in from the street and glimmered quietly to itself—almost like the echo of words in a language a person might understand, if only she had been raised in a world of glass and earth.

Maya fell asleep listening to the cabinet and dreamed what must be its dreams (things melting, things crumbling, things being made and remade)—and then woke up in the middle of the night, her eyes seeing nothing but darkness, her breath catching in her throat, all of her consumed by an idea the dreams themselves seemed to have given her: *She must save her mother!*

How do I do that? she asked herself. The thought had come to her so suddenly, ripping her right out of sleep, that she was somehow certain she *could* save her mother, if only she knew what she must do. The room was very dark and quiet at that hour; even the baby cabinet was slumbering away on its table, and a thin breath of sweetness came drifting her way from her books.

She sat up in her bed. That was it, of course: the *anbar*. How could she have not seen it? The *anbar* that brought people back to life—wasn't that what that desperate man had said? And the happy, beautiful woman they had met at the door of the Salamander House that first day, she had said something similar, hadn't she? Life! That was what her mother needed, most of all. Some of that radiance they all had, the beautiful people of the Salamander House. The brightness in their radiant eyes.

She was already at the bookshelf by now, digging the warm little case of *anbar* out from behind the line of books. Oh, it smelled lovely. There were flowers that bloomed only at night, weren't there? It had been calling to her, and she had taken so long to hear it. The round satin box nestled into her hand like something alive. She tiptoed into the kitchen with it and started going through the cupboards, looking for something that would tell her how this thing should be done. And then she found it: a small container of organic honey her mother had bought to put into her tea. Honey! That was perfect. Her father never sweetened anything he drank. And James did not even like honey. Perfect.

She took off the tops of the two containers very carefully and studied their contents. The dusky sweet smell of the *anbar* was now everywhere in the kitchen. The honey glistened peacefully in its jar. It was as if she knew now exactly what to do: The spoon sang out from the drawer, the hot water tap called to her from the sink. The heated spoon sank right into the golden *anbar*, and brought up what struck her as exactly the right amount (though of course there was no way of knowing), and then the *anbar* vanished into the honey as she stirred with the still-warm spoon.

After the lid went back onto the honey jar, she had another thought. She took a sticker from her school binder and wrote "ONLY FOR TEA!" on it with black ink, and stuck that on the honey jar. Just in case. And the honey went back into the cupboard, and the *anbar* went back onto its bookshelf, and Maya went back to bed, and her dreams the rest of the night were ordinary ones and slipped away from her as soon as her alarm rang in the morning.

10
SHIMMER

"Old photographs?" said Valko, taking a slow sip of his soda. He sounded, it had to be admitted, skeptical, and his eyes were still slightly sleepy, as an aftereffect of all those hours just spent in school.

The sun had come out again that afternoon during Histoire/Géographie, so Maya and Valko were huddled in their jackets around a table at the café. Pretending it wasn't actually October. Pretending also, at least in Maya's case, that if your mother is home from the hospital, that means life is pretty much back to normal. Even if "normal" means *anbar* on your shelves and a stack of bizarre snapshots you found hidden in the walls.

"Look at them, though," said Maya, and she poured the photos out of their old envelope onto the table. "They're strange, see?"

Even in the light of day, the long-ago children shimmered and glowed, the flat squares of those photos unsettled by some kind of illusion of depth, of color, of life.

"Oh!" said Valko, awake again. He picked up the nearest photograph and tipped it back and forth to watch the play of the light. "What *are* they? They almost look like holograms."

"You think that's what they are?" said Maya.

But Valko was already shaking his head.

"No," said Valko. "They couldn't be. They don't look quite right for that. Plus, I think you need lasers to make holograms. I saw this exhibit once—all right, never mind!"

Maya had actually managed to knock a spoon off the table in her impatience. The worry in her was getting harder and harder to bundle up and suppress.

"I just need to know what they *mean*!" she said. "You know why? Because remember that photo that Fourcroy guy took of us, when we were there with James? Remember that? Well, it looks *just like these*."

"No way," said Valko. He was really paying attention now.

"It's hanging up in his weird laboratory room. You and me and James. But James is the shiny one. He's shinier even than any of these. A really big number written on the bottom: 300-something. And something else about his being a Lavirotte. So here's the weird thing—"

"Numbers like these?" said Valko. He had found the writing on the back of the photos. "'174 X'? I mean, what's that, a kind of measurement?"

"It's got to be," said Maya. "The higher the number, the more the kid shimmers. See? Look at Adèle. 216. She's very shiny. But listen—"

"It's that camera!" said Valko. "I knew that camera was weird somehow. I was trying to see the brand name, and he kept getting in the way—"

"Valko, *listen!* He knew we're Lavirottes. How'd he know that? He was making a big show of being surprised we were relatives, and then all the talk was about him being a Fourcroy. So how'd he know—"

"Maybe the other guy told him. The old one. Hey, Maya, what's this date here?"

"But I don't think they get along at all. I don't think he'd tell him anything. I think this Fourcroy guy knew all along we were related—"

"1957? Could it be 1957?"

Maya looked.

"Could be. But you're not listening."

"*Adèle, 1957,*" said Valko, and gave Maya a meaningful look, as if she were supposed to get something from that. And then she followed the slow swoop of his eyes over to the Fountain of Lost Children, and she did get it.

"*Amandine, 1954; Laurent, 1955; Adèle, 1957,*" she

said, reading from that banner the cherubs had been holding now for more than fifty years. "You think this is that Adèle? Why? And I told you what my mom found out—they weren't really lost, those children. They went missing just for an afternoon, or whatever. They were just slow in the head. Or moved away."

"Don't know about *that*," said Valko as he bent back over those most peculiar photographs. "I mean, kids still go missing around here. That's what I've heard. They just don't get fountains anymore, right?"

Soon he had gone through the whole little stack of pictures, looking at the backs. Maya knew what he was looking for, and what he wasn't going to find: other names. Amandines or Laurents, for instance. He shrugged and let it go.

"So why are you worried about a photograph?" said Valko in his most reasonable voice. "Even a shiny one."

"Because I think he thinks James is special," said Maya. "He wants him for something."

And got stuck.

Because what she could not say (she could not even move her lips to form the words) was *he wants James to be the new Cabinet-Keeper.*

What she also could not say, almost not even to herself, was this: *And that's not fair.* She, Maya, was the one who knew how beautiful the Cabinet was. She was the one who would care enough to keep it safe.

"It all goes back to that Society of theirs, I guess," said Valko, filling in the silence where Maya had gotten stuck. "Philosophical chemistry and shininess. And fancy cameras."

He smiled at the photographs in a thoughtful way, his hands still tipping them back and forth: You couldn't help it, really. The light was so strange, the way it played in those faces. It made Maya feel sad and tingly, both at once.

"Don't you think—" she said, and got stuck again. "Couldn't it be—I mean, it looks to me like it, really it does—some type of *magic*?"

Valko looked at her. His eyes were such a comfortable shade of gray; you could almost see the thoughts in them, busily working themselves into actual words.

"They're kind of wonderful, right?" he said cautiously. "They're beautiful, these pictures. Is that what you mean?"

Maya shook her head. It seemed so stupid, when you said it out loud. She could feel her face beginning to flush, and she hated that feeling.

"It's just—all these strange things here. It wasn't like this in California. The salamander on that door. I swear it moves when it sees me. And our Cousin Louise—she's not just boring or whatever, she's actually really *hard to see*. And these pictures. They shimmer. It's not normal. It's not. It really has to be magic. I know I sound like an idiot."

And she *felt* like worse than an idiot. She felt like someone who had just torn off her nice mask and shown the whole world what an ugly, stupid dolt she really was. She stared down at the table in dull despair, her plain old doltish hand spread out flat and cold against the enamel.

"Hey," said Valko.

And his own warm hand settled right on hers for a moment, solid and consoling. Like there wasn't all that much to feel so doltish about, not really. Then the hand was gone again, but he was still smiling.

"You're not an idiot," he said. "You're just saying there are things here that you don't understand. That's all that magic means, right? Something real that nobody's figured out how to explain yet. There are nice scientific explanations somewhere, though. For everything."

"Even salamanders that turn their heads?"

"Well, only you saw that," said Valko. "So that one's pretty easy. Ninety percent of what we see is just our brain filling in the gaps. Really."

"Okay, then," said Maya. She was already feeling a hundred times better. She had taken a crazy plunge, and was still alive. That made up for a lot. "How about Cousin Louise? You met her."

"Hmm," said Valko. "Yeah. But I'm not sure I really remember much about your Cousin Louise. Sorry."

"That's what I mean," said Maya. "She's invisible. She's forgettable. She's hard to see."

"Doesn't sound like magic to me," said Valko, laughing. "Sounds like the opposite of magic. Too bad it's not catching—we could have her sneeze all over the dreadful Dolphin and his crowd."

Then he added in a different sort of voice—

"When is it, anyway, that big party of theirs?"

"What party?"

"The fancy-schmancy one. The Dolphin's thing."

"Oh, well, I don't know," said Maya. "I'm not going."

"Hm," said Valko. "Maybe you should, though. It's a way in, isn't it?"

"A way in?"

"I don't know. Maybe you could kind of sound out the Dolphin's gang while you were there. About that weird Society they hover around. About what their parents are all up to. We'd like to know, wouldn't we? You still have the invitation somewhere?"

It was still in her bag, in fact. They examined it together in the late-afternoon sun.

"Looks to me like you can bring a guest," said Valko. "You could bring me, for instance."

It was strange: She had taken that big plunge, yes, but half of her mind was still stuck, was thinking about the words written at the bottom of that glowing photograph of James, about the Cabinet of Earths, needing its new Keeper—and about the little cabinet she had made. How perfect it was. How well it had come out. All the tiny shelves were filled now with their miniature bottles of earths and sands. She had been thinking recently how nice it would be to hold the little cabinet up to the big one, to see how similar the two were. She could think that, but she couldn't say that aloud, not even to Valko. There was a lock on that part of her mind, and the lock itself was as hard to focus on as Cousin Louise. *It should frighten me more, being locked up this way*, thought Maya. But that was part of being locked up, of being stuck: She couldn't even look at the thing close enough to be frightened properly.

The other half of her mind was thinking: *the Dolphin's party! No way!* All those beautiful girls in their fancy dresses! She could just imagine their eyes narrowing as they looked down at Maya's sensible dark shoes, the ones her mother insisted were so good for ankles and insteps. It made Maya shudder, thinking of that.

"It might be sort of fun," said Valko. He smiled at her from under his slightly jagged fringe of dark hair. "You know? Apart from the research opportunities."

In the end she surprised herself: She said okay. Though she pointed out what it said on the invitation, about the strictly black-and-white attire; 8 p.m.; Palace of the Invalides.

Valko nodded. Valko agreed. And then he grinned and snapped his fingers.

"*Charismatograph!*" he said.

What he meant by that, Maya had no idea.

"That was what it was called," said Valko, pleased as punch to have found the word hiding in him somewhere. "That brand of camera he used. Not that I know what that means."

Maya's parents, unlike Maya herself, had absolutely no doubt that being invited to a party in a palace was a purely good thing.

"In the *Invalides*?" said her father, with a whistle of disbelief. "Dancing around Napoleon's tomb, or what?"

Once she had seen the invitation, Maya's mother actually took Maya shopping one afternoon for black-and-white clothes over near the Motte-Piquet métro station. They walked there slowly, both of them pretending they just preferred a nice stroll to a gallop, but really conserving Maya's mother's energy. It was a lovely day, the sky actually blue if you craned your neck back to take a look at it, and as days go it would have been almost perfect in every respect, except that Maya's mother kept bringing up Valko in a tactful, nonprying way, until Maya felt a little like screaming. Mothers can't help that sort of thing. But they found a nice skirt, white with black flowers. With her own white shirt and a black belt borrowed from her mother and her boring black shoes and her mother's black teardrop necklace, the Maya in her mirror on that Saturday evening looked more or less like someone going to a party.

Her hair was dark enough to go along with the monochrome theme, too, though not as dark as Valko's. It had grown out a bit since August, but hadn't yet quite reached her shoulders. (Back home, of course, her friend Jenna would have been there, those bluebird-blue eyes of hers sharper than any doubt or worry, to help Maya be fearless in front of that mirror: *Dude, not so bad!*) No, she didn't look a thing like Cinderella, and nothing she was wearing could pretend to be really chic, but all in all the effect was all right, she guessed. Then she caught a sweet whiff of *anbar* coming from the bookshelf and almost laughed. You'd think the stuff had a mind of its own, the way it was practically whistling her over. She pulled out the pretty case and twisted off the cover to take a look. About half the *anbar* hadn't gone into the honey. It sat there in its red case like some unbelievably fancy lip balm.

Well, she wasn't putting *anbar* on her lips. That seemed a little extreme. But she dabbed some behind her ears and rubbed the tip of her finger into her wrist the way old ladies do at department store perfume counters. Maybe that was a silly thing to do, but when the aroma of *anbar* wrapped itself around her, she felt, finally, dressed up. Not just dressed up, but, well, sophisticated.

And by then it was after eight and Valko was at the

door, all in black except for bright white laces on his sneakers.

"Like the look?" he said, showing off his shoes. "All the best spies are wearing fluorescent laces this year. That's what I hear."

Outside it was clear but cold, a nice October night if you had enough layers on or were on your way to a party where the rooms would be heated. They walked at a good clip, with their hands in their coat pockets, and Maya had the oddest sensation that she was rising slightly above the ground, floating perhaps half a centimeter above the sidewalk toward the floodlit golden dome of the Invalides.

"Well, here we go," said Valko as they approached the gate on the far side. "Good luck to us. Gather lots of data. You look totally beautiful, by the way."

But maybe she had misheard that. Maybe she had just made that last sentence up. By the time she looked up from digging the invitation out of her pocket, Valko was focused entirely on the great carved door they were about to go through, where a couple of burly guys were checking invitations and letting people in.

Inside, everything was grand in every way. Through one archway Maya caught a glimpse of long tables covered with desserts and bottles of soda. Another led to a room full of endless rows of coatracks. The ceilings must have been thirty feet high, the ceilings of a palace, and enormous chandeliers lit the stone walls and set the great windows glittering. In another large room the lights were dimmer and people were dancing. Mirrors everywhere. Beyond another arch she caught a glimpse of what looked oddly like stalactites. That made her grab Valko by the elbow and drag him back to take another look.

"There's a fake cave in this palace!" she said.

"Unbelievable," said Valko. "This is really unbelievable. Let's go dance. You know, to blend in, right?"

You can't wade into a dance. You have to jump in. You have to be willing to splash about like a spluttering fool. Maya took a deep breath and let go. There were lots of people dancing now, anyway.

She hadn't had a lot of good experiences, dancing, perhaps because worriers tend to get tangled up in knots when someone asks them to dance. But dancing with Valko wasn't like that. He wasn't worrying at all, for one thing. He was having a great time. And on his face was a friendly and conspiratorial grin, meant for Maya alone. *We're here together,* said that grin. *We're on the same team, and that's pretty great.*

It caught her by surprise when a strange hand settled on her shoulder, weighing her down. She looked up and saw the Dolphin leaning toward her, an interested, questioning look in his eyes, his nose testing the air.

"You're the *américaine* from school," he said. "Come

talk to me a moment. *Viens,* let's get something to drink."

Maya looked over at Valko, who made his dancing arms pantomime something that looked suspiciously like a person taking detailed notes in a *cahier.* She had to look away to keep her mouth from twitching at the corners, but the Dolphin's eyes were resting most earnestly on her. It seemed safe to say he hadn't noticed Valko at all. No, he was leading her—where else?—to the indoor cave, to a drinks table nestled between a pair of stalactites. He even poured out the soda for her, in a grave and aristocratic way. He was all attention.

"There's something about you," he said as Maya took a steadying sip of soda. "I noticed it at school one day. You're not like the rest of them. Who are you, if I may ask?"

He was really quite a good-looking boy, this Eugène de Raousset-Boulbon, with his shock of fair hair and his light brown eyes. He had very clear skin, too, as if he worked away at it with a loofah sponge every morning. Clear and soft. Ordinarily you aren't close enough to people to appreciate details like that. Maya took another hasty sip from her glass. Then something restless in her woke up and flicked its tail back and forth.

"Well, I'm Maya," she said. "I'm something like the niece of Henri de Fourcroy. Or the cousin."

She was surprised at herself, even as the words came out of her. They sounded almost proud, as if she were boasting. And a light came into Eugène's eyes when she said that. She had impressed him.

"Ah, I thought you might be," he said. Well, that made no sense. Why would anyone think she was related to anybody in particular, much less the purple-eyed man in the Salamander House?

"I've heard rumors," he added, as if it explained something.

"Oh?" said Maya. "Rumors?"

"That the Lavirottes had returned. You're a Lavirotte, I guess. And your brother."

"My grandmother was."

"So through her. *Bon*."

He was turning the plastic cup around and around in his hands, thinking about something.

"What do you plan to do?" he asked. Maya jumped. She had been watching the soda swirl about in his glass. "It's always the Lavirottes who change things. *Les vraies sorcières*. Well, and we need change, I'd say. They all say that."

"Oh, um, why?" said Maya, already out of her depth.

"You know," said the Dolphin. "The Old Man's rebellion. That's no good."

Maya was still trying to remember what a "*sorcière*" was, and now there was this Old Man to worry about, too. The old Fourcroy, maybe, with his miniature worlds in his boxes? But rebellion seemed a very strong word. She decided it might be best to head in some other direction.

"Tell me more about the *anbar*," she said, taking herself by surprise again. "Your mother said—I think I heard her say—it keeps her alive."

The Dolphin turned his head away from her very fast, but not fast enough. She saw the misery wash over his face. It seemed very out of place, unhappiness, shadowing all that smooth golden skin.

"My mother is immortal," he said.

She might have misheard that, too. She was always a couple of seconds behind in making sense of his French.

"Well, she's certainly very beautiful," she said.

"Yes," said Eugène. "My father, too. Have you seen him?"

Maya thought back to that day at the door of the Salamander House and nodded.

"Both of them immortal. That's very rare," said Eugène.

What could he possibly mean by that? It was all so surreal: this artificial cavern inside a palace, the soda bottles looking out of place under the plaster stalactites and trembling slightly with the beat of the music, the chandeliers glittering in the mirror-walled room beyond the arch. Maya's eyes flicked about her, resting for a single uncomfortable moment on Eugène's golden, shadowed face, and then retreated to the safety of the ice in her glass.

"But the thing is, they did it so young. Imagine! It was

right after I was born. And the Keeper was furious about it. He said they were too young. When he took their earths, he said they would be the last. Oh, your Uncle Fourcroy, the *Directeur*, he didn't believe him at first, but ever since: no. So that's when the rebellion began. There haven't been any new immortals since them."

He made a resentful sound.

"And then after that my parents couldn't be bothered much with ordinary things, like babies. Which are so much dull work. You understand."

Maya was pretty sure she was not understanding nearly enough.

"They couldn't be bothered?"

"Everything is very small to immortals. So far beneath them. Uninteresting. Gray. Only *anbar* gives things flavor, said my mother once when I was little. It's all she cares about these days. They should not have given their earths away so soon, I suppose. It's tiresome for me while I'm still left behind like this, of course."

"Ah," said Maya.

"You Lavirottes can fix that, though," he said. "Why can't I be immortal, too? You could stop the rebellion. Your uncle says—"

He bent so close to her that she could see that even his eyelashes were flecked with gold.

"He says the old Keeper has gotten out of hand. He's half-mad, apparently. And lives entirely in the past.

That's what I hear. Old and stubborn! Refusing to let new people in. Time for him to go. 'Someone younger and more flexible'—that's what your uncle said to my parents. And then he found you, the Lavirottes. Even if you had to come from far away. 'The perfect arrangement,' says your uncle."

His breath was warm and slightly cinnamony. He was so close to her now; she could not help but breathe him in. Even the melting ice in her glass trembled a little, though she was trying so very, very hard not to let it show, the tremor that was rumbling about in her.

"I see it now. The Old Man will never take my earth, not as long as he is Keeper. I'll never be immortal, if it's left up to him. But *you* could help me, you and your brother. The Lavirotte in you. You even look like her tonight. I didn't see it so much before."

There were more of his crowd in the room now, casting curious glances in her direction.

"I look like *who*?" said Maya, as a couple of the burnished girls cut away from the crowd and headed in their direction. "Who are you talking about?"

"The first Lavirotte. The first *sorcière*. Over the door of your uncle's building—"

And then the conversation changed because the girls were there, and there was more music, and more drinking and snacking, and from time to time she caught glimpses of Valko listening to people or chatting or bouncing slightly on the balls of his feet. She was never alone; the whole evening someone was always looking at her, or asking her questions, or just breathing in the air around her. She was somebody other than herself that evening, for all of those glamorous partygoers in their expensive shoes. And at the end of the party they all kissed her cheeks, in the cool French way. She hardly knew what to make of it.

"How'd you do?" said Valko as they went to look for their coats.

"Well," said Maya. "Let's see. Eugène's parents are apparently immortal, and he keeps insisting I'm a *sorcière*. I couldn't even remember what that meant at first, but then I did: a witch."

And the Old Man has rebelled—he won't put any more bottles in the Cabinet, she thought. But she couldn't say that aloud.

"It's that weird perfume you're wearing tonight," said Valko. "It's warping their minds or something. They were all buzzing around you like bees."

"Perfume?" said Maya, indignant for a moment—but then she remembered the *anbar* and stopped in her tracks. "Oh, right. It's that strong?"

"Overpowering," said Valko. "Apparently. Doesn't bother me too much, though, now I'm used to it. There's something in it that kind of fuzzes up a person's brain.

You didn't ask me how my research went."

"How'd it go?"

He gave a wry little shrug.

"Not very well," he said. "Nobody could tell me a thing about the mysterious Society. I am still in the dark. Their parents have appointments there. Or attend lectures. Basically I drew a blank. Did the Dolphin even mention the place? Or do we have to call him 'Eugène' now?"

"He wants to be immortal, too," said Maya, and was caught by surprise by a giggle. "Apparently I'm the one who could help him with that."

"Since you're a witch and all," said Valko.

"Yes, well," said Maya. "So I'm told."

And it was a strange thing, too: As the moonlight drifted down onto everything around them (the sidewalk, her hand, the surprisingly white laces of Valko's sneakers), she felt certain, somehow, that if that peculiar old camera were to take a picture of her just then, it would capture a different Maya than the usual one, an ever-so-slightly shinier Maya, a Maya all a-shimmer, for once, with light and depth.

11

WHAT CABINET-KEEPERS KEEP

The shimmer wore off, but the worry remained. Glass bottles and salamanders and phoenixes began appearing in the margins of Maya's math homework when she hadn't even known she was doodling. But almost as soon as the pictures had taken shape in her notebooks, she would be required, by whatever force it was that made her think of these things but forbade speaking of them aloud, to hunt through her pencil case for the big eraser, and remove all traces of bird, beast, or bottle. Clearly, the little cabinet was losing its patience.

But finally there came a Wednesday when Cousin Louise felt it made more sense to stay home and nurse her cold than come over to drill Maya on her French grammar.

"Well," said Maya's mother as she hung up the phone. "That's too bad."

Then she had to pause and cough for a moment: The cold was going around.

But Maya had already slipped into her room and was packing the little cabinet into a shoe box.

"Maya?"

Thwap! Down went the cover onto the shoe box, snug and tight, and secured for extra measure by a couple of pieces of tape.

"Maya?"

Her mother's head poked into the room.

"What are you up to? Did you hear? That was Cousin Louise. She can't come—"

"Okay. I'll be back pretty soon," said Maya, heading down the hall. "Got some errands. Sorry, Mom, I'm kind of in a rush."

She really was. She felt as though she must hurry, hurry, hurry, now that the chance was here. She ran all the way to the métro station, and tapped her fingers against the side of the shoe box while waiting for the train, and ran again from the Odéon station to the round green door on the rue du Four, and pushed the buzzer like someone crossing the finish line at the end of a very long race.

"*Oui?*" said that quavery voice, and then when Maya went into her explanation, her words tripping over each other as if they, too, were in some terrible hurry, the voice broke into the audible form of a smile.

"But of course!" it said. "The little cousin from California! Please, come in!"

He was already standing in the open doorway when

she came jogging into the second courtyard. The old Fourcroy was even smaller and older than she remembered; as she hurried forward to his doorway, she saw him run one trembling hand through his thin gray hair. The Old Man, that's what Eugène had called him. She could see why, and it made her feel a little protective of him, even now as she rushed forward those last few paces to where he stood waiting.

"The little cousin!" he said again, when she finally reached him and stood there, gasping for breath as she held her shoe box close to her chest. "Maya is the name, am I right? Come in, come in, my girl. I did hope you might come back."

"I wanted to show you something," said Maya, still fairly breathless after all that hurry. "Something I made."

They were in the studio now, and light came whispering in through all the windows, and the hundreds of little figures in their elaborate boxes seemed to lean forward to watch. Maya put the box on the table, undid the tape, and tugged at the lid.

"I made it," she said again.

There was a moment of utter hush as the old Fourcroy bent his head over her shoe box and lifted out from it the little cabinet with careful, tender hands.

"Ahhhh," he said, more an exhalation than a word. "How beautiful it is. My dear girl! Practically perfect, is it not? Your clever fingers! Oh!"

But it was strange: There was a struggle going on in that face. It was awash with awe—and it was so very sad. Sad!

"I tried to get it right," said Maya, suddenly feeling shy. "Do you think—is it right?"

And her eyes wandered over to that other door, the one in the back wall. The Cabinet was there: very close. Impatience welled up in her again, just like that.

"Please, I really need to know if I got it right. Can we go see now?"

He looked at the little cabinet in his hands, and he looked at her with his oddly tender and grief-stricken eyes.

"It is true, then," said the old Fourcroy. "I thought it might be. It wants you, *ma cousine*. It has brought you a long way already. And here you are!"

He showed no signs of moving toward that door, Maya noticed. She shifted from foot to foot, waiting.

"You have made a most beautiful thing, my dear," he said. "The call must be very strong in you, to have made something as lovely as this. And you look so much like my grandmother. That I saw right away, yes! But you are very young."

Why was he hesitating? Not just hesitating, but holding back. Maya could feel the rest of her patience evaporating.

"Please," she said. "I just came to see the Cabinet of Earths."

He had spoken almost in a whisper, but Maya spoke

aloud. She could speak to him. She could speak here. She could say what for some reason she couldn't say anywhere else. It was like part of her had been in a tiny, tiny cage all this long time, and now was finally free.

She took a step toward the inner door, just to see what the Old Man would do. He looked uncertain. He looked unhappy. And, at the same time, full of expectation: *thrilled*, somehow. It was a very disconcerting combination. It made no sense.

"Of course you have," he said, and even his words seemed to be wrestling with each other, as if YES and NO had gotten into a mortal battle in his head and his mouth. "Of course! And the Cabinet of Earths wants you, my dear! I just would like to ask: What do *you* want?"

"I want to see if I got it right."

She was almost glaring at him now.

He looked at her another second or two, and then gave a little nod, giving in.

"I'm afraid I have not been very strong," he said. "It seems quite possible, my dear—it is my hope—that you will be stronger than I have been."

And he led her into the other room, where the glass-fronted Cabinet rose up very tall and bright in its corner. She had remembered it well, she saw right away, and still there were things she had not remembered or had perhaps not noticed the first time: the brass berries peeking out from beneath the phoenix's spreading wings; the words etched into the curving line of the frame. She stepped forward another pace or two to look, while the old Fourcroy knelt down to set her little cabinet on the ground.

"I didn't see the writing before," she said, turning her head to follow the line of text as it sidestepped the small brass feet of the salamander and began making its way back down the Cabinet's other side. What did it say?

"Nothing is lost."

Well, that didn't seem quite right. As far as she could tell, there were in fact altogether too many lost things in this world: friends too far away, pretty green rings that you got on your sixth birthday and accidentally dropped down the drain the same day. Not to mention everything in the past. The feel of Boofer's soft puppy ears under your hand, the mint ice-cream cone you ate at the beach last summer, the voice of your grandmother on the phone—all as lost to you now as that poor plastic ring. Weren't they?

She turned to the old man, who had lumbered back up to his feet, his eyes traveling fondly between the big Cabinet and the little one, the little cabinet and the big one.

"Why does it say that?"

"Ah, well," he said, as if abashed. "They took one part of the truth, you see, and made a spell of it. Because they loved beauty, I think. You see how beautiful it is."

The Cabinet was beautiful, that was true. The way the frame wound so tenderly around the glass, the way the earths shifted, restless and lovely, in their bottles: It was not just beautiful, but truly *perfect*, the sort of object you might reach out to in a dream but could never ever hope to find standing against a real wall in a real room in your real life.

"Yes," said Maya, all the little wrinkles of doubt beginning to fade away in her brain. "I see that. It's beautiful, and it's real. Why should things always get lost? Why shouldn't some really beautiful things be kept forever?"

The brass salamander on the top of the Cabinet turned its head to look back at her. And smiled.

"Well, yes," said the old man with a sigh. "There is that. There's always that."

She lost track of his words, then, because the Cabinet was moving.

Moving? No.

The glass was melting.

No.

She turned her face away in alarm, and saw the old man looking at her, his worn face full of kindness and awe.

"How much you look like her!" he said. "*Ah, oui!* I saw it right away!"

"Something's wrong," said Maya. It was hard to speak. "Help me."

If she looked back at the Cabinet, the swirling glass would pull too hard. It would eat her up.

"You're the one it wants, my dear," said the old Fourcroy. "It wants to have you. Not whatever stupid young thing *he* might care to put in charge."

It was so hard to look away from the glass. Her neck ached. Her shoulders hurt. She had to force her head to stay turned in the Old Man's direction.

"I was even younger than you," said the old Fourcroy. "So much younger, yes. My grandmother led me to the glass. Oh, I didn't know! She was so sad, my *grand-mère*. The earth spilling out of her mouth! I was frightened! The glass in my soul! I was too young to understand."

Maya was filled with the strangest jumble of thoughts. She knew, for instance, that she should really be very afraid, but for some reason the Cabinet drowned out that fear. It could do that, apparently. It could open its great glass mouth, and a person could be falling into that maw and still be almost not afraid.

But Maya hung on, all the same. Not out of fear, exactly, because she really was almost not afraid, but out of something like stubbornness. Even the Cabinet could not just swallow her up that way, without her knowing what she wanted to know.

"Your grandmother shouldn't have done that to you," she said. "Without you even knowing. She should have made the Cabinet leave you alone."

"Ah, well," said the Old Man. "I was too young, but

she was in despair. She had lost her son, you see—my father. I think the Cabinet would have come into his hands, in time. That was how it was supposed to be. But instead, my uncle betrayed him, during that terrible war, and my father was killed. The curse of the Fourcroys, *ma fille*! They betray their brothers."

"He was jealous," she said. The plain truth, but to say it she had to fight very hard. Even just opening her mouth was hard, with the beautiful, hungry Cabinet pulling at her that way. "Your uncle was jealous, I guess. That's how it must have happened."

She did know something about jealousy, after all.

The Old Man looked at her.

"My father hid people here," he said simply. "During the war. People the Nazis wanted to find. Some of them just children, if you can imagine! His very own cousins, at one point. Here and at the Alchemical Theater. There are hiding places there. And then my uncle found out and was angry. No, not just angry—"

The old Fourcroy shielded his face for a moment with his hand.

"He was furious. It was risking the Society, risking all their work—that was what my uncle said. Too much risk—so he turned in his own brother. That's how it happened. And my grandmother despaired. She no longer wanted to live forever, not in a world where one son could kill another."

"To live forever?" said Maya. That was about how many words she could manage. She was still trying to listen only to the Old Man. She was still pretty stubborn.

"Well, yes," said the Old Man. "She had learned to put death away. She had made the Cabinet, after all! She was a true Lavirotte, like you—"

"Davidson, actually," said Maya, because it fed the stubbornness in her, and only stubbornness kept her from turning her head toward the swirling glass of the Cabinet, where the beautiful, precious earths hummed to her from their bottles and jars.

The old Fourcroy didn't hear her, though, or was too caught up in his thoughts to understand what she was saying.

"But then she despaired and took her bottle out. I saw it all, *ma fille*. Your earth comes finding you, once it's out of its bottle. It will crawl across half the world if it has to. It moves very fast. I was frightened then, believe me! I cried and cried, but she had despaired. The Cabinet must not go to my uncle, she said. I must be Keeper, though I was really too young."

He looked at Maya, all that sad history, layer after layer of it, deepening the lines of his face.

"Ah, how much you look like her! They made a statue of her to gaze down at the world from above the door of that house they built, the year my uncle was born. My terrible, beautiful uncle. How long ago it all is now. And now the Cabinet comes to you."

Maya gathered her strength together as best she could.

"Why to me?" she said. "Why should I agree?"

But she knew at the same time that she already had the answer to that question, too. Why else would she make a little cabinet and bring it here? Why would the call of the earths in their bottles be so compelling, if she wasn't meant to respond? Of course she belonged to the Cabinet of Earths! Of course! Not James! Her! And yet this tiny knot of stubbornness remained in her.

"Do you have a grandmother?" asked the Old Man suddenly.

"Not alive," said Maya.

"Ah, sad," said the old Fourcroy. "Because you could have saved her, if she were still living, you know, and you were the Cabinet-Keeper. The earth of her: mortality. Extracted, bottled, kept safely away. They do that, you know, in their Society, extracting the earths. They have an hourglass there—a wonder. And then they bring their bottles here, to be kept. Forever and ever, always the same. An immortal grandmother, you could have had. I had one once."

His eyes were distant now, like lakes on a foggy morning, when the shore fades into the gray all around. But even as the old Fourcroy became mistier around the edges, clarity and strength began to return to Maya's mind. The Cabinet had caught her off guard, with its swirling glass, but now an idea was growing in her, a larger idea than she had expected to find in herself. The dizziness was almost gone. She still kept her face turned away from the Cabinet, but it was easier now to look where she wanted to look, and to open her mouth and speak.

"Even someone who had been very sick?" she asked. "Could we bottle up the earths of someone who used to be sick? Or might still be sick? And then she would not be sick anymore?"

"Life!" said the old Fourcroy. "That's all that's left in them, the immortal ones. They cannot be sick. How could they be? No mortal part left in them to wither or fade."

Oh! Maya's heart filled right up and spilled over. She held her head high and stood up again, tall and strong against the pull of the swirling glass.

"Then I'll do it," she said. "Yes—"

The Cabinet roared in triumph behind her, roared and reared up and came rushing over her head like a great wave breaking on a rocky shore—

"—Just, not yet."

The wave froze, wavered, melted away again into a tangle of angry whispers. Maya turned around to face all that rippling glass.

"Not yet," she said again, still very strong.

The Cabinet was so beautiful. Nothing so beautiful had ever chosen her, out of all the people in the world, to be its Keeper. She put her hand on the glass, which was glass again, and not liquid, though it was warm under her fingers and still vibrating very slightly with the echo of all that it had so very recently been.

"For her, I'll do it," said Maya. "You know. For my mother."

At that the spell seemed to relax its hold on her, or at any rate the Cabinet of Earths, having more or less gotten what it wanted, sank down quietly into its corner and rested, and the old Fourcroy looked at it and at Maya with the oddest mix of expressions on his face. And then he shook himself as if waking up and went into his little kitchen and made them both cups of tea, which they drank at one of the worktables in the studio, with the ordinary light of day spilling over them from all those many windows.

"You'll have to tell them about my mother," said Maya, a little shyly. "They have to take the earth out of her. You'll tell them that, right?"

He looked very puzzled for a moment, and then his eyes sagged a little at the corners with worry.

"Maya," he said, giving quick, watery glances to the left and right, almost as if he feared that someone or something might be hiding among the decorated boxes, listening in. "Maya, my dear. Come outside a moment. Come this way, right outside—you can bring your tea!"

Outside! She felt foolish, standing in the courtyard with a teacup in her hand, but the Old Man was so anxious, his hand so full of tremble, that she worried most about him. And whether, perhaps, he might actually be a little bit mad, after all.

"Listen, Maya," he said in a whisper, his fingers gesturing back toward the place where the Cabinet stood. "Forgive me, dear girl, but the nearer I am to *it*, the more I find I forget certain things. Important things!"

His hand went anxiously through his wisps of white hair. For a moment he looked quite stymied.

"What things?" said Maya, to help him along.

"About grandmothers," he said, with a tiny gasp. "I mean, immortal grandmothers. I understand! I do! Of course we want our grandmothers to be immortal!"

"My *mother*," said Maya firmly. "Not my grandmother. My mother goes into the Cabinet of Earths. Or her earth does, anyway. In a bottle, like the others. That's the deal. She gets to live. Like it says: *Nothing is lost.*"

"Ah, yes," he said. "Of course, of course. But it's just—are you sure? It may not be—it seems to me—just to think about it some more, my dear. I mean, '*Nothing is lost'* is perfectly fine, as far as it goes. But also: *Everything changes.* They cut that bit out, the Fourcroys, when they started mixing magic into their science. I'm just trying to say—"

And he was trying very hard! There were little beads of sweat on his pale forehead, and his fine tufts of white hair were beginning to sag.

"—I'm just trying to say, it may be hard, my dear, for the poor grandmother, being immortal."

"Not my grandmother," said Maya. She was beginning to lose her patience with him. "My *mother.*"

He had paused for a moment, gasping for air, so Maya forged on.

"Just tell me what I have to do, to get her earth into a bottle. Because that's the deal: She gets to live. If the Cabinet wants me to be its Keeper—all right. Whatever. I will. But she's saved. You tell them that."

"It's you who must tell him, Maya," said the Old Man, in a thin, watery echo of a voice. "Of course you will! You'll tell him that, the head of the Society, the Director, the foremost Fourcroy, the Henri I was named for: my beautiful uncle. Brave girl!"

"Who? Who? Who do you mean, *the foremost Fourcroy*?"

Maya nearly kicked the wall in impatience. How many people with the same strange name could there be in one single city? Did she have to go looking *again* for some ancient, unfindable Henri de Fourcroy?

"Even the young one in the Salamander House is a Henri!" she said. "That man with the purple-blue eyes. And now you're saying there's another one, too?"

"Ah, *ma fille*," said the old Fourcroy, his eyes fading again into mist and distance. "My poor, dear girl! But that Henri de Fourcroy is not another one at all: It is he! Himself! He, my dear, is my terrible, beautiful uncle."

12

AN UNLUCKY FAMILY

It happened three times in a single day: Maya reached to open a shop door, and a frowning face loomed at her from the glass. Her own face. Maya Davidson, future Keeper of the Cabinet of Earths. By the third time, she was so rattled by it, she just slouched right away without buying anything at all.

Because you'd think that a person who had just more or less arranged for her mother to be saved from death would be in a pretty good mood, wouldn't you?

Well, no.

Instead a terrible restlessness had gotten into Maya's bones. She sat down in a chair, and then it felt like time started pouring past her, a flood of wasted time, and she would leap right back up again, while her mother looked up from her book in surprise. It was like she'd forgotten to do something, and then forgotten that she'd forgotten it. Like there was a list somewhere of things she urgently needed to do, and time was running out, and she had lost the list.

"Maya!" said her mother, putting the book she was reading down on the table. "You're acting like a trapped cat!"

At the same time she was happy: That was the odd thing. Like right now, looking at her mother, her face, her warm and loving eyes: to think she was going to be *all right*, after all. Forever and ever. Well! All those fancy doctors hadn't been able to manage it, had they? They hadn't loved her mother nearly enough, that was the thing.

You had to be able to love things, to save them. You had to see the beauty in them, the way the brass vines of the Cabinet wound their way across the glass, the bottles curled so tenderly around their dark handfuls of earth—

"Speaking of cats," said her father, looking up from the letter he was reading. "The neighbors say Boofer thanks us for the lovely shirt. Why is our dog thanking us for articles of clothing? Did we send Boofer a shirt?"

"Boofer's not a cat," said James.

"I didn't say he was," said their father.

"You said, 'speaking of cats.' "

Impatience sent the pen in Maya's hand skittering to the floor.

"All right, that's it," said her mother, laughing a little. "No more homework! You need a break. And for your information, Greg, I did send Boofer a shirt. Why not?

An old shirt of Maya's. It had a hopeless snag in it."

They were all looking at her now, but Maya's mother was smiling that particular smile of hers, the one that meant she had done something nobody else's (sane) mother would ever do, and was not embarrassed to admit it. On the contrary: was rather pleased with herself, and enjoying the joke.

"Well, I was going to throw it out. But then I thought: a postcard! For Boofer! All the lovely smells of Paris! Maya's school, the bakery, our apartment—I'm sure for a dog it's all there. So I stuffed it into an envelope and mailed it off."

"Cool," said James.

Boofer! That hollow homesick place in Maya's heart contracted for a moment—and then she thought about Mrs. Johnson, in the house next to theirs, opening an envelope from Paris and pulling out *Maya's dirty old shirt*, and all the impatience and irritation came flooding back over her, and her chair made an angry scuffing sound against the wooden floor.

"Oh, Maya!" said her mother. "You poor girl. Leave those books and go walk around the block or something. It's almost five, anyway."

At five she was supposed to meet Cousin Louise.

Cousin Louise!

But she did not want to see Cousin Louise. Some part

of her really, really didn't want to see Cousin Louise.

In fact, so much irritability was crawling about under her skin that when her mother leaned over to give her a kiss, Maya actually flinched.

"Maya, what's up with you? Something wrong? Tell me about it, dear."

"I can't," said Maya. "I'm sorry. I'm late. I can't"—and the impatience pulled her like a very taut string, right out of the apartment and down the stairs.

Because there it was, the source of all that impatience and irritability: She knew now—she knew!—she could save her mother. The thing is, when you *can* do something, you get itchy, you get impatient, you feel you *must*. Before time runs out, or the tide changes, or the train leaves. And there were things she had to do, or it was all no good. Going back to see the *foremost Fourcroy*, for example. It was awful, but she had to arrange things with him somehow, for her mother. After that, it would be all right. The Cabinet was waiting impatiently. The Cabinet was beautiful, and it would be all right.

And no one could know anything—anything—about it. She could not say a word.

She was late for Cousin Louise, who was sitting alone at her café table, no coffee before her yet. Of course. The waiter wouldn't even come by without Maya there; that's why Maya was always so careful to show up on time. Until today.

Her bad mood had swallowed her up. She poked at her drink viciously with her spoon and wouldn't even look up at Cousin Louise for the longest time.

"Well," said Cousin Louise eventually, her voice as level as ever. "I gather you are no great fan of the *passé simple*. Nevertheless."

I am being unreasonable, thought Maya, but somehow she couldn't stop being unreasonable. Unreasonableness seemed almost to be pouring into her from elsewhere, into her and through her and drowning out everything else.

The purple-eyed Fourcroy. He was the one who could take the mortality right out of a person's mother, extract it, and bottle it up. And then it would be Maya's job to keep that bottle safe, Maya and the Cabinet of Earths. . . .

"—Fourcroy," said Cousin Louise. Maya looked up in surprise. Cousin Louise seemed to have been speaking already for some time.

"Not as young as he seems," said Cousin Louise. "I've thought it over, and I'm sure. Our unlucky family! Always the same man. Can it be? Untouched by time, eternally young—"

"Immortal," said Maya, and then her mouth clamped shut, and she couldn't speak at all.

"Well, now," said Cousin Louise. "Immortal? That seems very unlikely."

How had the word even slipped out? Because it was definitely a slip. It was almost talking about the Cabinet itself, to say something like that. Maya sat up a little. Something was waking up in her, something buried underneath all the static of her unreasonably bad mood.

She looked up at Louise and made the only sound she could make at that moment, a sort of tight-lipped hum.

"Maya?" said Cousin Louise.

And Maya took the bottle her drink had come from and held it up like an idiot, right in front of Cousin Louise's face. And made that foolish sound again.

"Maya, no need to grunt," said Cousin Louise. "The word is *bouteille*. Noun, feminine. And in any event, please don't wave the poor bottle about. You can put it down."

"Yes," said Maya. She could speak about soda. "Yes, exactly. *Bouteille*. F-f-f-f—"

But there she got stuck again.

"Fourcroy," said Cousin Louise, and though it was hard to tell, she seemed almost to be thinking about something.

The waiter, misunderstanding, had already brought another bottle of soda, and had, what's more, ignored Louise's instructions to take it back. Maya put her finger on the bottle, on the cool beads of water condensed on its side, and thought very hard about soda so she wouldn't get stuck again.

"So. You are saying: the *immortal* Fourcroy," said Cousin Louise, and she leaned back a little in her chair. "Did I get that right?"

"Yes," said Maya, patting the bottle of soda, just to be safe. "Thank you."

And then they ran through some verbs, all the same.

Maya was still sitting there mulling things over after Cousin Louise left—just noticing that the irritability had let up a bit, like an ache once you finally take the medicine your mother keeps offering you—when she looked up and saw Valko coming her way and smiling.

"Hey, have some of this," she said to him, and pushed the extra bottle his way.

"What's up?" he said, plopping into Cousin Louise's chair. "You look pretty thoughtful."

"Families," said Maya. "Heredity. You know."

"Test isn't until next week," said Valko.

They were studying genetics in their biology class. Maya had tried to force her way through the biology textbook, but it was a hard slog. And her mind kept wandering off.

Let's see. If your great-great-grandfather's sister is, say, a witch, and then data is missing for a few generations, and then your mother is clearly not a witch, though admittedly a little bit quirky around the edges, and then experts in the area of witchness tell you *you* are a witch, even though the only evidence for that so far is making miniature Cabinets of Earths and nearly being swallowed alive by the big one—well, the only solid genetic conclusion you can draw from all that is this: *magic is recessive.*

But what about luck?

"My Cousin Louise says we're an unlucky family," said Maya to Valko. "Do you think that's possible? Unluckiness is a trait, like brown hair?"

"Brown hair is very lucky, though," said Valko. "Keep *that* in mind."

Maya took a final sip of her soda and shook her head at him.

"Seriously, though," said Maya. "Look at everything that happened to Cousin Louise's family. Squashed by a church! And before that, the war! And now, the way she lives. So maybe she's right."

"We-e-ell," said Valko, settling back in his chair in a comfortable way. "What do you think? Do *you* feel particularly lucky? Or unlucky?"

That was so much exactly the problem that Maya could only stare at him for a moment while a sudden storm went twisting and howling through her mind.

"I don't know," she said.

Because that's the thing: How can you tell? If your mother gets cancer, that's bad. But if she gets cancer and so far is still alive, what's that? Lucky or unlucky? It feels so very much like it must be one of those things, luck or unluck. Only you just don't know which. Not yet.

And then the Cabinet, too. Or being a Lavirotte. How could she know yet whether she was lucky or unlucky, to have been chosen that way by the Cabinet of Earths? All of those things tangled together.

Her hands were hanging on to each other so tightly her fingers ached.

"But some people are luckier than others. You know, like my brother," she said. "People just want to help him or be around him. And you know what—I did feel lucky the night we went to that party. Like everything in the universe was pretty much on my side, for a change."

Valko grinned at her.

"Surprisingly fun, that party," he said. "As far as the science of luckiness, though, I don't know. We'll have to keep thinking about that one."

Indeed. There was only one way to figure out for sure whether the Lavirotte branch of the Davidsons was genetically unlucky: research.

"Hey, Mom," Maya said that evening. "Tell me more about Louise's family. About what happened to them during the war."

Her mother looked surprised for a moment, and then sighed.

"Oh, Maya, they all died, I'm afraid. During the war,

when the Nazis occupied France. It's a terrible story, really! The father was a Jew from Argentina, the mother I think had some role in the Resistance, if the stories are true, and in the end they all died—except for Henriette, of course, who grew up to be Louise's mother. Henriette survived because she went to live with her cousin's family, with your grandmother, that is, out in the countryside somewhere. But her parents, her baby sister, they were hiding with relatives in Paris. Someone turned them in. And all three of them died."

An unlucky family, thought Maya. She felt sick inside, imagining that little girl Henriette, far away, not knowing where her family was, never hearing any news, and all the time having to pretend nothing was wrong, out in that village with Maya's grandmother.

"How come you never told me any of this before?" she said.

"Because it's so sad," said her mother. "It's hard to have to admit to your own children, when they're little, how sad the world can be."

"It's not just sad," said Maya. "It's awful."

Her mother traced a thoughtful pattern on the tablecloth with her finger: a loop that faded very fast into tentative wisps, into nothing.

"I guess it's up to us to save what we can," she said finally. "That's why my mother tried so hard to adopt

Cousin Louise, I think, after the accident in the church. There wasn't much of the family left. Maybe someday it will be your turn to be brave and save someone you love. Who can say?"

Maya's mother stood up because the buzzer was ringing; James and his father were back from the park.

"Well, and that reminds me that I've been intending for ages to invite Cousin Louise to tea—"

So there it was. The impatience washed back over her, rising like a prickly tide: Maya *had* to go back to the Salamander House, however hard it might be. Because given this strange chance of hers, she could not, could not, waste it: She had to do *whatever it took*, if *whatever it took* might save her mother.

But there was a slight problem with that: Her brain kept rebelling.

She would get as far as the avenue Rapp, and then something would happen—she would remember some other errand she had to run, or her mind would flash back to what it was *really* like, sitting in that living room with the young Fourcroy looking at you with those purple-blue eyes. And once she was at the intersection, hesitating a little, and there, suddenly, was the friendly face of Valko.

"Hey there, Maya," he said. "What's up?"

"I've got this errand to run," said Maya, but she could

feel her resolve crumbling away.

Valko waited a moment.

"Yes?" he said. "So can I come along?"

In Maya's whole life, only her crazy dog Boofer had ever looked quite as hopeful and expectant as that. It was like some leash suddenly snapped, pulling her right out of her sorry mood. She couldn't help herself: She smiled.

"I wish you could," she said. "But it doesn't matter. I don't think I can do it now, anyway."

Valko gave her a sharp glance.

"No?" he said. "Then you want to come along with me? I'm not going anywhere in particular. My feet just wanted a walk."

They walked down the rue Saint-Dominique, past bookshops and bakeries and the thick-walled church with maybe the best name in Paris ("Saint Pierre of the Big Pebble") and all the way to the open grassy spaces of the Invalides before Maya could even really say anything at all. But Valko didn't seem to mind. He seemed perfectly comfortable to be strolling along with Maya at his side.

Whereas Maya's mind was a dusty jumble of worries. She wanted to talk, she needed to talk, she longed to talk, but there was just so much she couldn't—*could not*—say.

She said, "It's about my mother."

"Oh," said Valko, and for a moment he even put a sympathetic hand on her shoulder. Just a moment, but the warmth of it kept spreading through her. "Is she doing all right?"

"I don't know," said Maya. That was the truth. How much more she could say, though, she didn't know. All she could do was dive in, as best she could: "But that's why I have to do this—I have to go back to that Fourcroy, the one in the Salamander House. He can help her. I have to get him to help."

They were across the wind-blown lawns of the Invalides, back in the narrow street again, passing bars and art stores and government buildings. Valko stopped in his tracks for a moment, his eyes widening with surprise.

"Wait a second. What's *he* have to do with anything?"

"He can help my mother," said Maya.

"How? Because he's rich?"

Maya looked at him unhappily: She had reached the edge of what she could say. It was like walking right into a wall. And on the other side of that wall was Valko, friendly and kind and deserving better than this.

"It's not about money," she said. "I have to go ask him something. I wish I could talk to you about it. But I just can't."

Valko gave her another look, and then the little street widened into a boulevard, and people with shopping bags began jostling by. He moved a little closer.

"Okay," he said. "But you know he's creepy, right?

You should take me along."

"I wish I could. I wish I didn't have to go at all. I wish I could explain it all so you'd understand."

"Hey," said Valko. "It's your mom. Of course you feel bad."

So then she had to root around in a pocket for a tissue, and that slowed them down for a while, but when her eyes were clear again, they kept walking. It was easier, somehow, to be moving along the sidewalk together. It's a lot harder to feel awkward and stuck when you're walking.

"At home you must have friends you can talk to," said Valko.

"Well, yeah," said Maya. "There's Jenna. She's really great—you'd like her. She's always so clear about everything. I mope, but Jenna knocks sense into me. And then there's my dog. He doesn't mope, either."

"I don't think you mope," said Valko. "Hey, look where we are."

They were by a very old fence. And through it, you could see the remains of some ancient structure, crumbled walls and all. And another building rising in Gothic swoops above the ruins.

"See? You know what those are? Roman baths. Thousands of years old. From before Paris was even Paris. And on top of them they built that medieval building there. It's a museum now. But you know what?"

He pointed through the bars of the fence.

"My theory is that that's kind of like me."

"What?" said Maya. She figured she'd heard it wrong.

"Well," said Valko, grinning again. "I'll tell you, but if you laugh at me, I'll cry. So here's my theory. You know how I was born in Bulgaria and then lived everywhere else on the planet, a few years at a time? Every time I move somewhere new, it's like starting all over. New language, new school, new friends, everything changes. But somehow it's still me, just a mixed-up, composite, mish-mashy me. See? It's like those buildings there: the current Valko, the older Valko, and somewhere under everything, *the ruins of Bulgaria*!"

Valko's hand punctuated those words with a great swoop through the air, and his other arm gave Maya's shoulders a hug, and all in all, Maya felt better, just at that moment, than she had felt in days.

"Getting late," he said. "And there's still the whole walk back. Need to make a call on my phone?"

Maya's mother didn't believe in cell phones. Well, that is, she believed they existed, all right, but she also believed her children shouldn't have them until it had been absolutely, definitively proved that cell phones did not cause cancer.

"I think I'm okay," said Maya. And inside her there

was an exclamation point on that: *Okay*! Because just for that minute, anyway, she really was.

It still had to be done, though. She still had to talk to the purple-eyed Fourcroy about hourglasses, bottles, and saving her mother.

The next afternoon she actually tripped over the shopping bag of the old lady slumped on the bench nearest to the salamander door before turning tail and starting to walk away, her heart dark with frustration

But someone was calling to her, so Maya stopped in her tracks and turned around. It was the old lady with the shopping bag Maya had just tripped over.

"Oh," she said, guilt leaping up in her. "I'm sorry!"

It was a very ordinary old lady, a slumped and bland little creature with pale eyes and gray hair. But she did not seem too angry about the bag Maya had knocked about. She was staring at Maya, and something in her face, in the blandness of it, reminded Maya of something.

"Why do you want to go in there?" she said to Maya. "You keep walking by, and stopping, and walking by again."

"My uncle lives there," said Maya.

"They are wicked people, the ones living in there," said the old lady in her dull and inconsequential old-lady voice.

"I'm sorry," said Maya again (about the bag). She had

turned to go, but that nagging sense of seeing something familiar held her back for a moment. "Why do you say that?" she asked all of a sudden.

"I know they are wicked," said the old lady. "They did this to me."

But her hands didn't so much as twitch to give an indication of what the "this" that had been done to her might be.

"Now I've come back to Paris, though," said the old lady. "Everything in it has changed in the last fifty years, believe me. Except them. I came here to see."

"Oh," said Maya. Tomorrow she would have to be braver than today. Tomorrow she would have to come striding up to the door here and go in, absurd or not. She picked at the snag at the edge of her thumbnail, trying to smooth it all out, and the old lady shifted her weight a little on the bench and kept talking, as old people sometimes do.

"—The chair may even still be there," the old lady was saying. "Who knows? Stay outside, stay safe. Better that way."

"Oh!" said Maya, the old lady on the bench before her suddenly snapping into focus. "The chair? What chair?"

Because now she knew what it was about the dullness of this dull old woman that seemed so familiar: She was another one of them. She was another (though older) Cousin Louise.

"They come in and go out and don't even notice me now," said the old lady. "No one notices. I am invisible."

"Not to me," said Maya. Fifteen seconds ago: yes. But not anymore.

"Ah, *ma fille*," said the old lady. "I once was a child like you. Perhaps just a little younger than you, back then—1954, it was. Long ago. Be careful, little one. Keep your life and your bright colors. Stay outside."

"Why?" said Maya.

"Such a charming child, that's what I was," said the old lady. "*Come in*, they said. Why? Why did I go in?"

She sat still on her bench, waiting, it seemed, for Maya to answer her old unanswerable question.

"Why did you go in where?" said Maya. "This building? When?"

The old lady shrugged.

"I was hit by a car, you see, to start with. Yes! A car came rolling over me, right here in the avenue Rapp. And yet—*miracle!*—I was fine. They saw it happen. They had a camera in their hands. They brought me inside and put me in their beautiful chair. Things carved into it, you know. Creatures. Birds. Was I frightened? I don't remember. And then they took it from me."

"What did they take?"

"It, it," said the old lady. "All I don't have now. I was charming, before. People saw me, you know, and smiled. I was very lucky, *ma fille*. Like you."

"I'm not so lucky," said Maya, but the old lady shook her head.

"The car rolled over me, and I stood up and laughed! A miracle, a little miracle. But then they took me in and sat me in the chair and took it from me and put it in a box," she said.

"Took *what*?" said Maya.

"I told you that already," said the old woman, and her face seemed vaguer again. "Didn't I? What I had then, before. All the charm and the luck in me. What you still have, you fortunate child. *What excellent* anbar *this will be*, they said to each other. *How a little dose of this will brighten our endless days! Truly,* anbar *is the food of the gods!* Oh, why did I go inside? And ever since, my dear—"

Horror prickled its way down Maya's back.

"*Anbar!*" she said. "Oh my God! But I thought it was something to make sick people well."

The old woman just shook her head again.

"Wicked people. Wicked people. It was long ago, when they ate me up that way. I was Amandine then, you know. And now who am I? Tell me: Who am I now?"

In that one awful second, Maya lost all of her French:

It just went away. She had been wrong. She had been terribly, terribly wrong. *Anbar* saved nobody. It was just the food of the gods. A treat, a drug, a snack. But the price of it! Oh! She took a step away from the old woman on the bench, a step toward the door of the Salamander House, because by then she was remembering another thing, the most terrible thing of all.

"*They took it from those children!* But Cousin Louise! And you were Amandine! But—I put it in the honey! Oh my God, my mother!"

Her lungs, her heart, they were filled, at that moment, with a cold so deep she could have screamed from the sheer pain of it: That is what fear feels like. She had gotten mixed up. She had been wrong. It had never been *anbar* that made people immortal: It was always only the Cabinet of Earths. And she turned away from the bench and ran, as fast as she had ever run, down the avenue Rapp, across the rue Saint-Dominic, as fast as she could, all the way home.

13
AN ISLAND FOR LAVIROTTES

In French the word for picture is *tableau* (noun, masculine).

And when Maya came bursting into the living room of her apartment (five minutes and thirteen seconds after leaving the old lady on her bench outside the Salamander House), this is the *tableau* she found:

— Cousin Louise, sitting very straight on the plain, gray couch, a napkin dangling from her hand;

— Maya's mother, leaning forward from one of the hard-backed chairs, just starting to pour out a glass of tea;

— the faces of both Cousin Louise and Maya's mother, turned toward the crashing entrance of Maya and frozen as if by the flash of a camera, all surprise and alarm;

— the gray tangle of steam threading its way up from the teapot's spout;

— a plate of cake, all in slices;

— and the opened honey jar.

"Stop! Don't!" said Maya, and she flung herself forward toward the coffee table so violently that a lurching arc of tea splashed right onto the sleeve of her coat. It didn't burn at first; the fabric just sagged against her skin. "You can't! Don't touch it! In the honey—*anbar*!"

She was not fast enough. While her mother set the teapot back down with a clank and grabbed for Maya's damp sleeve, Cousin Louise whisked the honey jar off the table and brought it up to her nose.

"In this?" she said. "Is what?"

The back of Maya's hand was beginning to sting, but she reached out with it anyway, making a desperate grab for the jar. But for all her dullness, Cousin Louise could move very quickly when she wanted to. The jar in Cousin Louise's hand stayed just out of Maya's reach. And then Cousin Louise did something so shockingly unlike herself that Maya and her mother both gaped at once: She stuck her papery finger right into the jar, scooped out a glob of honey—oh, the smell was sweet, even from where Maya stood; her heart galloped a little, just to have that thin tendril of sweetness reaching out to her that way, and her mother, next to her, gave such an odd little sigh—and Cousin Louise pulled her honeyed finger out of the jar and stuck it right into her mouth. Like a child. Not just any child. Like a badly behaved (as the concierge might say) *American* child.

But she kept her back very straight as she did it. Her back was straight and the expression on her face was entirely unreadable, her finger in her mouth all the while.

"Hey, I want some of that, too!" said James, appearing in the living room so suddenly it seemed like he must have teleported himself there from his bedroom. "What's that? I want some, too!"

"Oh, don't!" said Maya again to Cousin Louise, but her voice was already not much more than a worn-out croak. "Don't do that!"

"You don't even like honey," said Maya's mother to James. And then: "Louise, are you sure you're all right? Maya, calm down!"

Cousin Louise stood up in one sudden motion, a stern column of Louiseness, with the honey jar still open in her hand.

"This came from *where*?" she said.

"From the organics store on rue Cler," said Maya's mother.

"From the Salamander House," said Maya, under her breath.

Cousin Louise shot her a sharp look.

"I'll take it along with me, then," she said. "So sorry, Sylvie. I am late."

They had shown a movie like this in art class, once: the vague pencil sketches to start with, and then the artist's hand coming to ink things in, to make them definite.

Every possible edge of Cousin Louise seemed one notch inkier than Maya had ever seen before. And then the new, ever so slightly more definite Cousin Louise screwed the lid back onto the honey jar and started walking to the door.

"How much of that honey did you have?" said Maya to her mother, though she had to run after Cousin Louise before her mother could answer, had to catch up to the swiftly retreating Louise and put her hand on her arm to slow her down.

"Wait, Louise—I put *anbar* in it," she said, in a desperate muddled mumble. "Don't eat it. Don't. The way those people all want it so badly—I think it's addictive. I think it's a drug. And it comes from—oh, you mustn't eat it. Please don't."

"I remember the scent of it," said Cousin Louise. "How extraordinary! I remember everything now."

And with that she went out the door into the hall and away.

Maya looked after her for one puzzled, miserable second and then went back to the living room, where her mother was toweling up the puddles of tea and letting James eat two pieces of cake at once.

"Maya!" said her mother. "What on earth is wrong with you?"

"That honey," said Maya, still drowning in miserableness. "How much of it did you eat?"

"Maya!" said her mother again. "You come barging in like a crazy person, nearly break the teapot, practically throw yourself at Cousin Louise—"

Maya sat down on the couch with a resigned thud. The back of her hand was really smarting now, where the tea water had scalded her.

"I just wanted to help," she said. "That's all."

Her mother gave her a very odd look and then reached forward and took her hand in hers.

"I'm sure the honey was fine," she said. "It's not something that goes bad, you know. Not with all that sugar in it. And anyway, I never even got to taste it, the way you came storming in."

She gave Maya's hand a squeeze meant to be reassuring, but Maya had old ladies on benches and Cousin Louises and her mother's odd look swirling around in her head and was not exactly reassured.

With good reason, as it turned out. Because there are certain rules followed by Thoughtful Mothers around the world when you let something slip (and nearly breaking the teapot while shouting incoherent warnings about honey did count, Maya had to admit, as *letting something slip*): They take you somewhere, that day or the next, to have what they like to describe as a nice, comfortable talk. They say things like, "We haven't had a chance to catch up in a while, have we?" They mean well. And if there's really nothing at all in your life going on more serious than tomorrow's history quiz or needing new shoelaces, who knows? Maybe your heart doesn't sag right into the pit of your stomach when your Thoughtful Mother suggests going out somewhere, just the two of you, right now or possibly Saturday. To a museum, said Maya's mother. To the Louvre. *Wouldn't that be nice?*

"I'd like to show you what I've been doing with myself, all these weeks, while you're at school," said her mother.

"All right," said Maya. What else was she going to say?

So Saturday, right after dropping James off for his half day of school (only the little kids had school on Saturdays), Maya and her mother took the métro across the river to the Louvre, which turns out to be connected to an immense underground mall, with record stores and clothing shops and everything you can imagine, so that by the time they came to the entrance of the museum itself, Maya felt just a little bit encouraged. Surrounded by shoppers, it's hard to think your happiness hinges on some bottle filled with earth in a cabinet somewhere. And so far her mother was chatting about this and that, more like a normal person than like a Thoughtful Mother, though her movements were slower than they once had been.

But then they were riding escalators up past statue

after statue, and the crowds thinned out, and the air became quieter, and Maya could almost hear her mother steeling herself up for full-on thoughtfulness, for indirect questions, for everything that makes comfortable talks such, well, torture, usually.

But instead her mother sighed and smiled. Almost a mischievous smile, to tell the truth!

And she said,

"There's a painting here I want to show you."

The wooden floors squeaked underneath as they walked: *squeak squawk squeak squawk*. It would be hard to sneak into the Louvre and steal even a little statue or an enameled plate without anyone noticing. Well, they probably have all sorts of modern alarm systems up everywhere, too, but the floors do a pretty good job on their own. Maya took two or three steps on tiptoe, just to see if that helped, but the floor squawked underfoot all the same. And then her mother stopped before a medium-sized square painting on the wall in front of them and pointed.

"This one," she said. "Do you see?"

Maya rolled onto her toes and back down (*squeak*), catching enough of a look to get the idea: cute baby Jesus bouncing on his mother's knees; lots of rich red cloth; some man kneeling before them with about the worst haircut the Middle Ages ever saw.

"Believe it or not, I grew up with this picture," said her mother. "My mother had it in a book. She was always showing me the river, the garden—"

Maya took another look: There *was* a river there, winding into the background, between vineyards and hills, towns and cathedrals. All cleverly framed by those three arches at the back of the room or chapel. And two magpies in the garden.

"The little people walking over the bridge—do you see them? In my mother's book you needed a magnifying glass to make them out. Tiny little people walking to heaven. The other side of the river, where the pretty churches are. Left bank, earth; right bank, heaven. See? But my mother said—"

Maya's mother stopped to take an extra breath or two, and Maya made a note of that in the secret record book she was keeping inside her head: how her mother was winded by the trip up to the top floor of the Louvre, even though it had all been escalators, just about. Not even stairs.

"She said what she loved about this picture was that even the world in it was beautiful. Not just heaven, she meant. The other side of the river, the mortal side. See, look, Maya! The green, green vineyards sloping down to the water. The mountains far away. It *is* beautiful, isn't it? I hope those little people appreciate it all properly."

Maya put her nose closer to the painting, but the little people remained very, very tiny, carrying their tiny flags over that faraway arching bridge. Hard to tell whether they were appreciating the scenery properly or not.

"There's a boat on the river," she said, now that she could see it all better. "And an island with a castle on it. How'd he paint it all so small?"

She looked at the name on the label: *Jan Van Eyck. c. 1390–1441.* Well, that was ages and ages ago. Days probably felt pretty long in the fifteenth century. Not all that much to do. Time enough, anyway, to spend hours dotting paint onto your canvas, one hair's worth at a time, until the little banners could be carried into the heavenly city.

"The island," said her mother. "Yes, I know. What's an island doing there, in the middle of the river? You know what my mother used to say?"

Maya remembered certain things about her grandmother very well: the feel of her dark blue sweater, the pearls that hung from her ears like tears, the slight smell of lavender and thyme that made her different from other people's grandmothers. And when she laughed, she used to tip her head right back and become, by some trick of the voice, about a hundred years younger, just for a second.

"She used to say: That's ours; that's where we live, the

ones in our family. A little bit of us always not here, not there: on the island in the middle. Between the worlds. An island for Lavirottes, she used to say. That was her family, you know. Ours, too."

Maya looked at the little island rising up so gaily above the winding river that was apparently supposed to be death, and she felt an odd twinge of resentment. Maybe not every Lavirotte was happy being *not here, not there*! Maybe some Lavirottes just wanted to be normal!

"It's just a painting," she said.

"Yes," said her mother. "But I like it very much. When I was sick, I used to think about that island in the river, and how a person could climb the tallest tower and look out at the beautiful fields on one side, and the golden towers on the other side, and the tall mountains in the distance all around. And then, who knows, maybe go down and find a boat and just row yourself right over to one bank or another."

She paused.

"And now I like it because it's beautiful."

Sometimes you have to barge in, thought Maya. *Sometimes you can't just wait for the hints to fall crumb by crumb into your outstretched hands.*

"Mom, if you were sick again, would you even tell me?"

Maya's mother made a funny sound, a little hum of surprise, but she didn't say anything.

"I didn't think you would," said Maya. "You never tell me anything. Why can't you just tell me? I really need to know. I'm old now. You can't just keep me in the dark forever."

"But, Maya," said her mother. "All those tests, remember? As far as I know, I'm fine."

Still, there was something veiled in her expression. Those lucky-unlucky Lavirottes on their islands! How could you ever tell with them?

Her mother looked at her watch.

"Oh, look at that: We have to hustle if we're going to get back in time for James," she said. "Let's just loop back downstairs past the Italians on our way out."

By the time they were on the métro again, Maya's mother looked pale enough that a man offered her his seat. Maya stood next to her, swaying as the train wound its way back under the Seine, and her heart felt raw somehow, as if it had been scalded by spilled tea or exposed slightly too long to an open flame.

They took the escalator up to the street level when they got to their station, and still Maya's mother needed a few seconds at the foot of rue Cler to catch her breath.

"Want me to go pick up James?" said Maya. "We'll meet you back home. Maybe I'll even take him to the park or something. No need for you to rush around."

"Good idea," said her mother. "Go!"

So off Maya ran. But she went the slightly longer way, through the park, to look at the bare trees, to help her heart get itself back into order. And then when she came racing up to the door of James's school, there they all were, the parents, the children with their after-school pastries and cookies, the boys running around and shouting, the dour old guardian at the door, who would have looked entirely in place perched on a barrel at harbor's edge by the sea somewhere—there was even a dent in his nautical frown where a pipe was clearly meant to go. The only thing missing from the scene was one brown-haired five-year-old in a steam shovel sweater. James was not there.

She waited a while, picking at an old callus on the ball of her left hand: Sometimes the kindergarten class came down late, if they had painting supplies to put away. But as the knots of children and parents began to dissipate and wander away, Maya saw she had no choice. She went up to the guardian with his dented frown and asked where her brother was: James Davidson, Kindergarten B.

The guardian's whole face rearranged itself into a wrinkled smile. The young James! Quite a fellow! But *mademoiselle* must not worry, James was already gone.

"On his *own*?" said Maya. Irritation washed through her, cold in her veins. How could they let him run off like that by himself! And with all the traffic on the avenues, between here and home. Oh, he should have known better—

"But no, *mademoiselle,*" said the guardian, the dent in his smile becoming deeper and merrier. "Not alone, of course. An outing, yes? James went away with his *uncle.*"

14

TIME!

Almost before she had fully absorbed that terrible, dreadful word—*uncle*—Maya had already started running. She ran so fast she could not even feel the pavement underfoot.

When the really bad things happened to Maya—

when her mother had said, all those years ago, "Okay, so it's a tumor, but they're going to do what they can";

when they called from the hospital to say her grandmother had died, and her mother just stood there, holding the phone, and couldn't let go;

or, for instance, *now*—

she froze, yes, but not the way other people freeze, not by standing still, not by losing the ability to move or speak. Maya froze into a colder, faster version of herself. Her mind got smarter and colder. Her fingers got colder, too. Her toes got so cold they just vanished from her inner sense of herself. The world became very simple, in a chilly sort of way.

She ran all that long block to the door of the Salamander House and hesitated only a moment under the sad stone eyes of the Lavirotte witch: calculating what she should do next; working out what she might say.

Someone was calling her. Not by name. Someone was saying, "Hey, you there! You girl!"

She spun around, her fingers itching to tap in the code and get on with it. It could only have been fifteen minutes, after all, since the purple-eyed Fourcroy had led James away from that school. Fifteen minutes. Or twenty, max.

The old lady who had once been Amandine was rising up from her bench. Maya must have run right past her a second ago. She called out to Maya in her thin voice and stumbled forward, almost tripping over her own feet in her hurry to reach her.

"What are you doing, *ma fille*? I told you! I told you! Don't go in there—"

"He's taken my brother!" said Maya, a wild flow of words. "That Fourcroy in there with the purple eyes!"

"Ah!"

The bland old face stiffened slightly, as if rage might somehow break through the vagueness of her.

"Ah, c'est terrible!" she said. "My poor girl! But when?"

"Right now!" said Maya. "Fifteen minutes ago! I'll get

him back! I'm going in!"

And she was just turning back to the door when the bag lady grabbed her arm.

"He's not in there," said the old woman. "I've been on my bench, two hours already, watching. Nobody's gone in there, not the last half hour or more."

Maya stared at her for a moment, her quick, chilly mind spinning its many, many little wheels.

"Then where is he?" she said. But even as she said that, she knew where James must surely be: "An outing," the guardian at the school had said. An outing where? What kind of outing? A trip, perhaps, to the second courtyard off the rue du Four? To the place where the Cabinet lived?

Because that was what that purple-eyed Fourcroy had actually wanted all along: a new Cabinet-Keeper, *somebody younger and more flexible*. Someone he thought he could keep under his thumb. And Lavirottes! He had wanted a Lavirotte! Yes, all the pieces were falling together now. He had arranged it all, the fellowship, the coming to France, all of it, just for that: to get a Lavirotte, but one he could control. Oh, James was too young—but the Old Man had been even younger, back when his grandmother had given him to the Cabinet.

And this terrible knot of bad feelings tightened in her chest: How could James be made Cabinet-Keeper? He was so little! It was a terrible thing to do to someone as young as James. And besides, the Cabinet had chosen her, not her brother! Hadn't it? And she had been going to save her mother! The thought of the Cabinet, the beautiful, shimmering glassy mystery of it, with its bottles and shifting, restless earths, was suddenly almost more than she could bear.

The Cabinet would help her, she thought. Yes. The Cabinet wanted her to come. She had to get there now, right away, while the wild coldness still made her brave and fast. But first—

"You have to do something for me," she said to the old lady. "Please, will you do this?"

And she was scrambling around in her jacket pockets for a scrap of paper, for a pen.

"You know where the Bulgarian embassy is?" she asked the old woman. "Right there at the corner. You can just about see it from here. I need you to leave this note there for Valko. He lives there. Valko Nikolov."

He's taken James—please call Cousin Louise—she'll know what to do— parents don't know.

She copied out Cousin Louise's phone number from the emergency info page of her calendar and stuffed the paper into the old woman's splotchy hands and said "*Merci, merci*" and turned and ran again, to the métro this time, and then past turnstiles and through tunnels and in and out of trains and up a long flight of stairs into the daylight again, all the way to the round green door on the rue du Four in the center of Paris, to the rickety grounded tree house at the back of the second courtyard, where the wispy, worried face of the old Fourcroy rose up behind the window glass when she pounded on his door.

"But, my dear child!" he was already saying as he let her into the vestibule, and his hand was trembling as it brushed her cold, desperate cheek.

"Are they here yet?" she said. "Where is he? I have to stop him!"

"Stop him? Stop whom, *ma fille*?"

"That other Fourcroy! That Henri with the beautiful eyes! He's taken my brother."

The old man looked appalled.

"Your brother?" he said. "What do you mean, he has taken your brother?"

"I thought he would bring him here. He wants a new Cabinet-Keeper, you said that yourself. Someone young, someone he can boss around. I know he wants you gone. I thought—"

But already she was looking around and seeing such an absence of five-year-old brothers, such a gaping lack of evil, purple-eyed uncles that it took her breath away all over again.

"Oh, no," she said simply. "He's not here, is he?"

"No, my dear," said the old man. "He's not. He doesn't care to come here, so close to the earth that still dreams of him in its bottle. He stays away, as much as he can."

"But then where's my brother?" said Maya.

"I'm so sorry," said the old man. "I don't know. In that house of theirs, probably? Oh, Maya, *c'est terrible.*"

Terrible seemed like an understatement to Maya, just at that moment.

"But no one had gone inside! The lady said so. The lady on the bench. They can't be there. No one even went inside."

Though some other part of her was listening to all of this and already knew she had gotten it all wrong again. Not just wrong, but terribly wrong. As wrong as that awful, beautiful, horrible chair, as wrong as what had been done to Cousin Louise, to the poor old lady on her bench. As wrong as *anbar.*

"Through the Alchemical Theater, probably," the old man was saying. "There are so many passageways, you know, from one building to the next, so many hiding places. . . ."

And Maya had only been *five minutes late*!

She pounded her fist down on a worktable so hard that the little figures in their boxes gave tiny jumps of surprise. Then her hand hurt, and her mind cleared, and she grabbed the old man's thin arm.

"We can't waste any time," she said. "That's why I came here so fast. We have to stop him."

"Yes," said the old man. "It is time. It must stop. But my poor girl, you've hurt your hand."

He was right; she had. Was she supposed to start caring about a *splinter* now, with her brother missing and the world all askew? Maya yanked it out of her hand so roughly it began to bleed. Oh, what did any of this matter? They had to hurry now, that was the thing.

But the bead of blood on the side of her hand glittered a little in the light and stopped her: How perfectly round it was, bright red and beautiful, and even the windows all around were caught in it now—tiny perfect reflections of themselves.

"Maya," said the old man, his voice quite soft and far away. "What can I do to help you?"

"You're their Cabinet-Keeper. They have to listen to you. Tell him they have to let my brother go, *or else*."

"But I can't do that," said the old man. "I'm sorry, dear girl, but it's too far. When I was younger—yes, then, whole blocks at once! But the Cabinet binds you tighter and tighter with time. I can't go any distance at all, I'm afraid."

The perfect round pearl of blood was balanced on the side of her hand, waiting for something, and the Cabinet was waiting for her, too, just a few feet away.

"All right," said Maya. "Then we'll unbind you, right? Go! Tell him you are *not* Cabinet-Keeper anymore. Tell him Maya Davidson is Cabinet-Keeper now, and *she* wants her brother back right away. Tell him that. How do I do it, though?"

"It was very long ago," said the old man, a little shy. "But I think it's the blood. The blood, you know, and the glass."

He put his hand on her head a moment, a slightly trembly hand.

"I think maybe you will be stronger than I have been," he said in his rough whisper. "I hope you will."

My brother is only five years old, she told herself firmly. *We are not like the Fourcroys. We do not betray our brothers.*

She shut her mind to everything else. That was what she had to do. So Maya went through the doorway into the room where the Cabinet was waiting.

No time to waste. The air in that room was thick with urgency, with the pull of the Cabinet on her, with the hands of the clock in the corner straining forward, and, somewhere, her baby brother in the balance.

The Cabinet was so bright. The glass was shining; the shelves were shining; each bottle ablaze with its own particular color, its own unique brown or red or russety-amber, the earth within. Maya held up her hand in front of her eyes, just to block a part of that light, and the little bead of blood still clinging to her hand caught the Cabinet's reflected light and played with it, began to swirl and pulse. Everything liquid.

When she looked up, she saw that the glass was rippling, too, a vertical pool of light shimmering there before her. The illusion was so strong that she felt for a moment as if she were floating above a tidal pool, looking not forward but down, at shining bottles resting a few inches below the sea's clear, swirling surface. She put her hand out just like that, simply reaching out for one of the bottles, the ancient green one there in the middle, with the dark, dark earth in its belly, and at the moment her hand touched the surface of the glassy pool, a shock went through her. Because it wasn't water, after all. It was warm and slightly sticky; it flowed over Maya's hand, yes, but not the way water flows, or even something much thicker than water, like glue. It flowed with warmth and intention. Not just that: It welcomed her; it came seeking the bright spherelet of blood and the core of her, the blood melting into the pool of glass, the liquid glass beginning to make its way into Maya's veins.

There was a whispering in her ears. A whispering of shadows in the glass. They came flowing into her, too, their images, their voices: the Cabinet's keepers, now shadows woven into the glass itself. There was a frightened wisp of a boy cowering there, and another shadow, very strong, that came close to the surface and stared out at her, its glass shadow of a hand wrapping itself firmly around Maya's own. *At last,* said that shadow's face, old and beautiful both at once, and Maya knew it then: She had seen the same sad face carved into the stone above the door of the Salamander House. *At last, a true Lavirotte,* said the shadow. *A brave one, I think. At last.*

"I am letting him go," said Maya to the shadow in the glass. Maya meant the little wraith of a boy whose shadow was hiding now behind the brass phoenix in the Cabinet's lower front corner. Younger even than James when his grandmother had bound him to the Cabinet, very young to be caught in the glass that way, just flitting from one corner of the Cabinet to the next, peering out at her with his wide shadowy eyes. Something familiar about him, all the same.

"I know who *you* are," said Maya to the little one hiding there. "Come on out."

She reached for him (like reaching for a reflection in a pond), and then somehow he was there, a hint of surprised laughter running like a spark along her arms and leaping away. She turned fast enough to see the laughter still lighting up the old Fourcroy's face like a lamp. Laughter and surprise. He put his hands to his face, and for another second or two he still looked very young, for all that his face was covered with wrinkles and his hair was so wispy and gray.

"Now you run and tell him," said Maya to the old Fourcroy. "You're free now, aren't you? Tell him he must give back my brother. *Or else!*"

"Ah, yes, *ma fille*!" said the old man, his face still folded into that surprisingly youthful grin. He patted his legs as if they were gifts he had not seen before.

"All right, all right," she said. "Just go fast. Go fast and tell him. I'm the new Cabinet-Keeper, and I say he must leave my brother alone. Go quick."

"And you—don't be too long," whispered the old man. "Wait too long, *ma fille*, and you'll never, ever leave."

It was a relief when he was gone. She could turn her head back to the Cabinet, where her hand still rested in the pool of glass and the bottles waited, glowing. When you looked at them closely this way, you could see: The earths were beautiful. Not just the bottles and jars that held them, but the earths themselves. They had streaks of darkness in them; they were not any one pure color, but many things all at once, shifting and changing. She watched them for a moment, feeling thoughtful. So that was what you gave away, when you decided to become immortal.

Her eyes were sharper now than they had been before; perhaps they were adjusting to the light. But she saw now that the bottles had patterns in their glass, pictures and shapes that shifted themselves into something coherent as she looked. If she squinted a little and relaxed some corner of her brain, the patterns became as legible as names. She could see, for instance, that the bright jar on the second shelf belonged to a woman; when she moved her hand closer to it, the picture became clearer in her mind: not just any woman, but the one who had come stumbling out of the Salamander House, all those weeks ago. Eugène's mother. In her jar was a small amount of what looked like golden sand, shifting about restlessly within its glass walls.

That sand looked nothing, for instance, like the dark, complicated earth in the green bottle next to it. She knew before even passing her hand over the bottle whose earth that must be: Nothing else in the Cabinet was as old or as secret as this. That's where it rested, then, the mortal part of the purple-eyed Henri de Fourcroy, put into the Cabinet of Earths when he was still young and beautiful. How many decades ago must that be? Eighty years? Ninety?

The room became very quiet, just waiting for Maya, waiting for some great thing to happen. Even the sad, old shadow of the Lavirotte witch came rippling around to the front of the Cabinet, watching her and waiting, too.

Enough. Maya put her fingers firmly around the neck of the bottle, and pulled, but at first it would not budge, a bottle-shaped limpet clinging to its part of the pool.

Stupid bottle! But it had to come out: It was the one thing Maya could think of that could give her power over the purple-eyed Fourcroy. The one thing he might be willing to trade James for. She pulled and pulled, but the Cabinet clearly did not like to let things go.

"Oh, you should have done this yourself!" she said aloud to the shadow-witch watching. "He's bad. Why did you let him go on and on and on?"

He was still my own son, said the shadow.

(It didn't need words to say these things, of course. The glass flowing through Maya now carried shadow in it, too.)

I could not, it said. *I could not. And the Cabinet had bound me, though I was its Maker. I waited too long, and it bound me. You must work fast, Maya. Fast!*

The bottle came free then, and in one smooth motion Maya pulled it up to the surface of the Cabinet's glass pool and brought it out into the air and the world with the tiniest of little popping sounds, as if a bubble had been broken. Maya gasped as if she herself were just coming up for air, and at that moment the shadow-witch swam up to the very surface of the glass and looked out at Maya with something so like Maya's own face that it was hard to sort out what was shadow and what was reflection. Especially since the shadow then said what Maya had been thinking herself:

Quick now! Before the Cabinet has time to bind you.

A Lavirotte made it—a Lavirotte can end it!

"But my mother," said Maya, and she hesitated for a moment, worrying.

Of course it was evil, the Cabinet, for all that it was the loveliest thing Maya had ever seen. But Maya thought of her mother, and her heart was torn right in two.

On the one hand, her mother, well and beautiful—always well and beautiful, placed right out of reach of time and decay. That was what the Cabinet could do. Her mother, safe for ever and ever, exactly as she was now, always Maya's own mother, even decades and decades from now, when Maya herself might be old and gray.

Her mother—like the purple-eyed Fourcroy.

And that right there was what you might call "the other hand." Because her mother, her lovable, creative, ever-so-slightly extravagant mother, was nothing at all—thank goodness!—like the beautiful, unchanging Fourcroy in the Salamander House. What's more, she would not want to be like him. Never in a million years. So there.

And Maya stepped back from the Cabinet and looked around the room.

Don't do that, said the Cabinet. It said this by becoming even more beautiful and precious, every part of it gleaming with secret magic. *Wait a little, Keeper. We can save her, you and I. Wait, and you'll see—*

Hurry, whispered the witch's shadow in the glass. *Now. Time.*

"Be quiet!" said Maya to all of them, but mostly to drown out the images the Cabinet poured into her now. The old Fourcroy's tools hung on the wall by the door. She reached out blindly and grabbed the first thing that came to hand.

(The island in the middle of the painted river; her mother looking out from one of the turrets there; safe and sound, forever and ever—)

"Not fair!" said Maya, and she heaved the thing in her hands high above her head. A hammer. High above her head, and then her arm froze.

Because this is what the Cabinet was saying now: *Are you absolutely sure, Keeper? Are you sure?*

"Not fair," she said again, but her voice had slipped into that other world, the world of the painted island, the world where her mother was safe, forever and ever. She could feel the tug of that place on her, and the Cabinet's warm whispers spreading like worry through her veins.

I'm already a little bit stuck, she thought. There was some important reason why she should not get stuck, though she could not quite remember, just then, what it was.

(At that very moment her mother turned in her painted turret, in all that loveliness, and looked straight at her. And shook her head to get the too-perfect paint out of her hair.

Honestly, Maya, she said. *Stay here FOREVER? Without even a bridge or a boat? Are you absolutely nuts?*

And then the Cabinet raged around her in beautiful fury and took all the images away.)

Time! Maya, unstuck, swung the hammer forward as hard as she could, and the world exploded with a bright, splashing crash. It hurt too much to think, so she just closed her eyes as tight as she could and swung the hammer, again and again and again, while the sounds changed around her, the glass splintering like ordinary glass, the metal pinging and denting under her blows.

When she finally opened her eyes, she was astonished by the crumpled heap in front of her, a messy jumble of glass and metal, all dim and broken now, in the room's gray light. Specks of earth were wriggling away in all directions, already looking for the people they had come from, long ago. They were moving fast; they were crawling away under the door, like crumbs blown along by an invisible wind. Like ants gone wild. They would find their people again, the earths, and all those beautiful, golden faces would be part of time again. Would change. Grow old. And, one day, die.

A single old bottle, faintly green, stood undamaged on the floor beside her. Maya let the hammer drop to the floor, and picked up the bottle with numb, disbelieving hands.

It was the most beautiful thing she had ever seen, the Cabinet of Earths—and Maya had destroyed it.

For a moment she stood there, blank, just staring at the wreckage.

But now even the wreckage was changing before her eyes. The shards of glass had already lost their edges: Soon there was a shining puddle of glass on the floor, right there among twisted bits of brass fronds and broken leaves. The salamander was gone. The glass puddle gleamed and sighed and shrank, giving off wisps of steam as it went. Now it was no longer quite as big as a manhole cover—now it was only the size of a dinner plate—now it was an opalescent splotch no larger than the palm of her hand—

And she reached down without thinking and scooped it up, a warm circle of glass/not-glass against her skin. In her hand it stopped vanishing: it seemed almost to hold its breath.

"Glass is not a liquid," said Maya aloud. She was still half in a daze. The glass melted and remolded in her hand, teasing her, almost. So she took it over to the Old Man's workbench and poked a string through it: it wanted to be worn around her neck. It needed that.

And then the clock in the corner began again to tick. It was almost one, said the hands of that clock: one o'clock in the afternoon. One o'clock! One o'clock! That woke her right up: The purple-eyed Fourcroy had taken James a little more than an hour ago.

15

EVERY SINGLE DROP

She paused only long enough to stopper the green bottle with one of the Old Man's little woolen sheep. Then Maya hopped over the oddly determined trickle of earth still pushing its way over the threshold and ran back through streets, métro stations, avenues, parks, all the way to the Salamander House, the bottle in her coat pocket thumping against her hip with every step she took.

There was a crowd, a beautiful crowd, clustering around the entrance to the Alchemical Theater. A matinee, must be. Ha! The earths would find them soon enough. Maya tucked her chin down and kept moving. If the old Fourcroy was right, there were ways into the Salamander House from the back of the theater, but she would never be able to sneak past all those noses unnoticed. So she left the back door alone and went to the front, where the salamander handle turned to stare over its shoulder at her as she came panting up.

Nobody else was there; even the old lady was gone from her bench. She glanced up and down the street and then typed the code: 1901. The year that the building had been built; wasn't that what the purple-eyed Fourcroy had told them? The salamander was chilly now under her hand.

When she pulled the door open, still there was nobody. She didn't go toward the stairway doors this time, where the buzzers were. *Back doors,* she had been thinking. The Old Man had given her an idea.

Parisian buildings of a certain age, like the one she had been living in since August, have certain things in common: They have garret rooms under the roof where the servants used to live, back when people expected to have servants. And they have dark wooden staircases winding up to those rooms, somewhere behind the marble glitter of the front stairs and the lacy metal elevator shaft. And the dark wooden staircases have to connect the garret rooms with all the building's kitchens, so that the poor overworked girls from the country could come slipping down from their attics to their stoves and worktables without offending their masters' guests by using the same stairs. And the back staircases had to connect the kitchens with the rubbish heap, too, so that the country girls could make the chicken bones vanish neatly after dinner. "Like magic," Maya's father had said, when he took Maya and James on a sneaky expedition up and down their own back stairs.

Not really like magic, though, thought Maya darkly. *Nothing but magic is really like magic, when it comes right down to it.*

She slipped into the courtyard as quietly as she could, and there it was, in a corner by the row of green and yellow trash bins: a plain wooden door. And sure enough, it hadn't quite latched properly, when the last person had pushed through it with his garbage bags. One sharp pull, and she was in.

Bare wooden stairs make more noise than carpeted ones, but she went up as quietly and quickly as she could, counting the flights as she climbed: *two, three, four. . . .* By then she was panting. And out onto the fire escape for a moment; through another door, and there she was. Inside.

The room had been a kitchen a hundred years ago, but now it was a kind of laboratory and supply room. Sinks and beakers everywhere.

Her heart was pounding so hard she had to wait for a moment before peeking out into the hall. She tried to take very quiet breaths.

But there was no one in the hall, either. And it was definitely the purple-eyed Fourcroy's hall, the same hall

Cousin Louise had shown her weeks ago, only now she was farther down it than she had been before, and the apartment's entrance seemed very far away, like something seen through the wrong end of a telescope. She slipped out into the hall itself, feeling very exposed, and made her way up to the next door: nothing. A storage room. Everything still quiet. Oh, maybe there was really nobody here, maybe the apartment was empty, maybe this whole day had been some kind of elaborate, terrible false alarm—

And then from beyond the next door came a little sound, a small ghost of a snuffle.

She put her ear to the door, listening for whatever noises cousin-uncles might make, and heard nothing but that little snuffle again. Nothing uncle-ish about it at all. Too small for that.

All the same, her hand felt very alone as it reached out for the handle of that door, and she turned the knob as slowly and silently as she could manage, opening the door just a sliver at first, just to peek.

At first she saw only the afternoon light glinting back at her from those looping tubes of glass, those metal instruments arranged against the green walls, the silvery vines that crept up the sides and back of the beautiful, terrible chair.

Another little snuffle. She hadn't even seen it, at first:

There was a miserable splotch of darkness crumpled in that chair. All of that twining loveliness wrapped around a huddled little figure, its eyes tightly closed against the light.

"James?" she whispered. It was so hard to see, with all those funnels and tubes and wires so delicately snaking around that small head.

The splotch of darkness opened its dull brown eyes and looked at her. It was James. And yet—sort of not James, all the same. A shadowy James. A dull James.

She was too late.

And rage welled up in her, welled up and spilled over. She almost couldn't speak, she was so angry—at the beautiful Fourcroy; at the school's guardian, who had just let James go walking off like that, with someone calling himself an uncle; at her parents, for bringing them to this terrible, terrible city; and most of all at herself, Maya. Who always came too late. Who always did the wrong thing. Who couldn't save anyone, not even her brother.

She was pulling at the tubes and belts and funnels all that time, digging her brother out of all that mess. He didn't even complain as she yanked on him. Whatever those awful mechanisms were designed to do, they did it somehow without so much as a single wire breaking the skin. And yet some terrible change had been worked on her baby brother, all the same.

"James!" she said, hugging him finally, with all the fierceness of her despair and her rage. "Why didn't you wait for me?"

"Don't feel so good," said James, and he slipped right out of her hug onto the floor.

"Did they hurt you? Are you hurt? Where'd they hurt you?" said Maya, pulling on his arm.

James shook his head. He wasn't really resisting her; he just wasn't doing anything. "Tired. Leave me alone."

And he sagged over into a small uninteresting lump at her feet. Against the gray of the floor, he was actually—Maya's heart contracted—rather hard to see.

All right. Maya's life was over; everything was ruined. Her brother had been turned into a miniature Cousin Louise, and it was *all her fault*.

She felt the full hopelessness of all that, but below the hopelessness she found she still had a firm layer of something else, something that had come up from deep inside with the rage and the anger. She recognized it by now, that solid thing in her: *sheer stubbornness*, that's what it was. It could hold you up for a moment in a wobbly world. You could stand on it and get your head above water for a moment, just long enough to find something else to hang on to, maybe.

She lifted her head and looked around. The tubing that she'd pushed away from her brother's head still loomed in a glassy tangle above and to the side of the chair. (And on the shelf, waiting, one of those sweet little silk boxes, with silvery writing on the lid: *for Maya*, it said. *A gift*. Empty. Waiting. She couldn't waste time worrying about it now; she just slipped it into her pocket, while her eyes worked to make sense of all the tubing.)

From a step or two closer she could see how it all connected together, all those tubes and cylinders and mysterious silver containers. There—at the end of the tangle, the tube emptied into a funnel. And the funnel rested in the mouth of a clear glass cylinder, about the size of a coffee mug. And in that cylinder, a liquid, a pale, straw-colored liquid. She put her nose down near it, and it was faintly sweet.

It all reminded her of something. In the woods once in New England, when she was very little, she had seen a tree with a wooden pipe coming out of it, like a faucet, almost, and a bucket underneath full of what looked like water.

"Why is there water coming out of the tree?" Maya had asked her father, and he said it wasn't water at all; it was something called sap. And the sap would be boiled down until it was maple syrup for pancakes. See? He had her stick her finger into the bucket and taste it, and it was true: There was just the slightest hint of sugar to it.

So this, thought Maya now, was the sap that *anbar*

came from, before they did whatever they did to it to make it thick and resinous and powerful. A last drop eased out of the tubing and fell, with the slightest of *plonks*, into the cylinder. She reached out and picked up the glass with both hands.

"James," she said, turning around very carefully, so that the liquid wouldn't slosh. "Sit up! You have to drink this. Right now."

On the floor by that awful chair, James just shook his head.

"Right now! Do you hear me? *Sit up!*"

She risked one hand to haul James up a little by his shoulder.

"Drink this," she said, holding the glass up to his mouth. "Come on. Quick!"

"Don't want to," mumbled James, his eyes dull and tired. "Leave me alone."

Well! The anger in her came together into something very pointed and precise. She squatted down so she was looking right into James's slumping face and pinched his shoulder again to try to make his eyes focus.

"You listen to me!" she said to him, in the harshest, bossiest hiss of a whisper she had ever used on him in all her years of sistering. "I am NOT going to leave you alone, you dope! You drink this right now, or I'll be really, really, seriously mad. I will tell Mom on you. I will take that stupid windup clown I gave you, and I will *throw it in the garbage!* Sit up and drink."

James sat up a little. He did seem just a smidge more awake.

"Don't throw out the clown," he said.

"Drink this," said Maya. "See? It's nice."

He took a drowsy sip, and then sat up a bit more.

"Okay, I tasted it," he said. "You won't throw out the clown?"

"If you want your clown back," said Maya, making every word as full of weight and edge as she could manage, considering she still had to whisper, "You will drink this up. Every. Single. Drop."

"Okay, okay," said James, taking another swallow.

"More," said Maya. "Quick."

She had been so focused on James that she had hardly been paying attention to anything else, but suddenly she realized that she had been hearing a slow, tapping noise for a few seconds: the noise of someone somewhere coming up a long flight of stairs.

This room! That dreadful chair! James still sitting on the floor, with the glass tipped up at his mouth!

"Come on," she said. "We've got to get out of here. No—bring the glass, too."

James had put it back down on the floor as she pulled him up.

"I finished already," said James. He was quite awake

now, Maya noticed. There was something almost like light in his eyes again—a dim light, but still. And he was just the slightest bit more visible against the dull color of the floor.

"You bring it along," said Maya. "I want you to lick it clean."

He did smile at that, a halfway smile. And Maya took his hand and led him down the corridor, the way she had come: through the old kitchen and out on the fire escape for a second, where the back staircase was.

"Hey!" someone shouted at them from far away. Maya glanced down, and there was a fat woman in the courtyard below, looking up at them with an angry face. *Strictly not allowed,* probably, for children to go out onto the fire escape.

Maya dragged James into the back staircase and paused for a moment, listening. Yes, there it was: the door, many flights below, creaking open. Angry feet on the stairs. So that wouldn't work.

But there was another door out of this staircase, a door leading to the left, and when she tried the handle, it opened.

"Quiet," she said, right into James's ear. "Come on!"

Behind this door was a long wooden hall, a forgotten place, it seemed like. Empty rooms opened up on either side of it, and there were cobwebby doors that looked like they hadn't been used in years. At the end the hall angled sharply right, went down a couple of steps, and became dimmer. And at the end of that stretch of hall was another door, and another wooden staircase, wending its shadowy way up and down.

"Cool," said James, sounding much more like himself.

Maya squeezed his hand.

"Come on," she said. "Let's go."

They padded down that long staircase, down and down and down and down. Maya was trying to count the flights, but it was hard to be sure. Some of the landings didn't even have doors to break up the blankness of their walls. When Maya and James had come down what she thought must be at least four stories' worth of stairs, they found themselves standing before another door, a very old door, by the looks of it, with looping lines of metal hammered into it, another one of those graceful iron plants James had once thought must be—what had he said?—*squids*.

Maya eyed the door with some doubt.

"There are a lot of stairs in this place," said James, and he sank down onto the bottom step.

"No, you don't!" said Maya, hauling him back to his feet. "You do *not* get to quit yet."

And she pushed them right through that door—into yet another hallway.

Another world, you might also have said, from the plain wooden staircases and abandoned halls behind them: Here every inch of the wall, of the floor, of the ceiling was decorated with tendrils and birds, little animals peeking out. The lampshades were curling blossoms of metal and glass. All in all, a riot of unliving life. It made you feel uneasy, being surrounded by all of that frozen motion.

"There's got to be a way out," said Maya, keeping a firm grasp on James.

Well, at least there were doors on either side of the hall, and a larger one at the end. The exit, maybe? She pulled James down the hall very fast (all those carved and jeweled eyes were unsettling, somehow), and poked her nose through, just to see.

No, no exit here. Just a round room. Round? Yes, round. And steps led down into it, through concentric circles of wooden railings. Pews, almost, she thought. A little amphitheater. A very strange place.

"Wow," said James, and he slipped right under her arm and in through the door.

"Have you licked that glass clean yet?" said Maya, looking up at the carved branches winding their way across the ceiling.

She hadn't noticed the door closing behind them; she was already halfway down the steps, her eyes on the pillar that grew up like a trunk in the middle of the room.

"It's sticky," said James.

She flicked her eyes toward the glass in his hands.

"Well, if it's sticky, then there's something left in it to lick," she said. But the room was distracting her.

She was noticing things. The air, for instance, was very still. It was a different class of air than they had been breathing, even out there in the hall. This air felt suspended in place. It was holding its breath.

And the pillar in the center of the room rose up from a small platform of burnished wood. A place for a person to stand. And on the top of the pillar—at about the height of Maya's shoulders, maybe—was an hourglass. Elegant French words ran around its rim: "*Who Gives Me His Earth*," they said, "*Rules Time.*" Above her (she tipped back her head to look) the pillar began again, nearer the ceiling, becoming the great trunk of that great, outspreading tree.

And curled over the top of the hourglass and staring at her with amber, curious eyes, was a salamander.

You could see where your hands were supposed to go, on the sides of the empty hourglass. It was warm to the touch, and inviting. It pulled at something in you.

The room grew brighter.

There were birds hiding in the branches of the tree, she could see now. The birds were silvery and bright, and their wings shimmered as they peeked out from behind the leaves.

Leaning against one of the wooden railings, James sat licking his glass and watching her. He seemed far away, shadowy and small. Not as bright as the birds in their magnificent tree.

The salamander flicked its bronze tail and smiled at her, and there was a very small sound from the heart of that room, from the hourglass between her hands—a tiny, sweet chime of a ping. And then another. She looked down at the hourglass and saw—two grains of sand. No, not sand, of course. Earth.

"Maya," said the little boy on his bench far away. "I thought we were in a hurry."

Ping. A third grain of earth. How long does it take to become immortal? Not so long, maybe, when time itself no longer really even matters.

The little boy stood up from his bench and came down the stairs.

"Look, Maya," he said, giving her arm a tug. "It's clean now. Let's go."

The touch of his hand broke her concentration entirely. Her hand slipped free from the hourglass, and the air came back into her lungs and made her gasp. The sweetness of the light was gone, and the silver birds faded back into their branches and froze still.

"Maya!" said the little boy, all in focus again.

She stepped back and looked at him. James, her brother. What had she been doing? How long had they been in this place?

"My glass is super clean," he said.

Three grains of her earth in the hourglass—what had she done? She still couldn't quite breathe properly; she just took her brother's hand and pulled him up the steps, back into the corridor, and out of that motionless air, through a different door, and into another sort of space entirely.

Vast, noisy, dark, cluttered. Bright lights far ahead, voices, and glimpses of curtains.

"I know where we are now," said Maya. "We're backstage."

They were in the wings of the Alchemical Theater.

"Be really, really quiet," said Maya into her brother's ear.

Because a few feet away from them, on the other side of that rippling gray curtain, someone was clearing his throat and beginning to speak.

16

IN THE ALCHEMICAL THEATER

"Esteemed colleagues, scientists, philosophers, friends!" said the voice, a voice Maya knew all too well.

Maya pulled James down into the most hidden place she saw: behind some old rolls of scenery and a pile of boxes. From here she found she could actually see a sliver of the stage through the slats of the crate in front of her. On the stage a handsome young man was standing at a little podium; behind him Maya could see rows of dim ovals that must be faces, and bright dots in scattered pairs: eyeglasses.

Not just any young man, of course. Their beautiful, terrible cousin-uncle, Henri de Fourcroy. Oh, he looked very pleased with himself as he stood waiting for the audience to hush. Probably thinking of his beaker of raw *anbar* waiting for him upstairs. Maya clenched her teeth so hard they squeaked.

A moment later the house had already fallen completely still, everyone leaning forward to hear what the purple-eyed Fourcroy might have to say.

"On this most happy occasion, welcome!" he said. "We are honored today by your company. A very auspicious hour for our Society! For it is on this day each year that we gather to remember our history, our achievements, and our Founders—"

James tugged on Maya's sleeve.

"He was going to give me hot cocoa," he whispered.

"Shh," said Maya, but she was mad all over again, just thinking about it.

"—under the benevolent shadow of the very Tour Eiffel whose construction brought so many of our Founders together, now more than a century ago. There were those among the chemists and engineers whose minds soared higher than the tower, is it not so?"

A sigh of approval came from the dim shapes of the audience. James shifted with impatience, and Maya put a heavy hand on his shoulder to keep him still.

"For there are substances rarer than iron," said the young Fourcroy, lowering his voice for the sake of drama. "And there are places that science alone cannot go. It is not enough to weigh rocks and track the stars: Our Founders knew this. *Science alone* watches, observes, and measures; *science alone* is weak."

More murmurs from the crowd, and many nodding heads.

"Weak! And *magic alone* isn't much better. Silly

superstition and old ladies listening to the dreams of trees! What, we might want to ask, is the practical use of *that*?"

A faint ripple of laughter.

"But our Society was founded by a Fourcroy, and the Fourcroys have always understood that power lies not in *science alone* or *magic alone*, but in the careful harnessing of *both*. Our Founder was the inheritor of the greatest of chemists. And he married magic. And here we are!"

Cheers from the hall.

(James was tugging on Maya's sleeve.

"Do trees really have dreams?"

She clamped a hand over his mouth.)

"Over the course of one short century, our Society has done what no Darwin, no Newton, no brilliant but old-fashioned Lavoisier could ever hope to do—"

At this moment two things happened almost at once:

James gave another impatient wriggle, in the course of which the toe of his shoe kicked Maya so sharply in the shins that she yelped aloud.

And then, second, just as the purple-eyed Fourcroy was turning his head to see what, in the wings, could possibly be emitting *yelps*, a commotion erupted in the audience, and his head swiveled in the other direction again, away from the rolls of scenery and piles of crates and Maya's swiftly thumping heart.

The commotion turned out to be an elderly man waving his fist and shouting. He came into Maya's view as he pushed his way down the aisle, shouldering past people larger and better dressed than himself.

"I object!" he was saying, as he dodged arms outstretched to stop him, to quell him, to escort him out. "I do most strenuously and vigorously object!"

Maya's heart gave another wobble. It was the Old Man himself, looking even dustier and paler than usual, in this place so far from his tools and worktables.

The younger Fourcroy leaned forward and made a languid, stilling gesture with his hands, a sign to the audience that they should not be alarmed by this ruckus.

"What troubles you, old man?" he said, as if he had never seen the person before him in all his life.

The old Fourcroy stood at the edge of the stage now, the light falling so clearly on him that Maya could see how indignation was pulling at the skin of his face, making his eyes very wide and wild.

"*You*, speaking of *Lavoisier*!" he spluttered. "*You*, calling yourself his *heir*! But *he* was a man of science! He established the existence of elements! He explained to us combustion and respiration! He wrote treatises on fossils, white soap, mineralogy, prison reform, wheat flour—"

A disbelieving titter was beginning to rise from the audience.

Maya couldn't help gritting her teeth: Oh, Lord,

Lavoisier! Now how was he ever going to get himself back to the point?

The younger Fourcroy seemed to have come to a similar conclusion: His back relaxed; he leaned forward, listening to the old man's ravings with an easy expression.

"—No, *mon oncle*, you are no scientist! Poor science! Poor magic! In you, they are corrupted. In you, my uncle, they become treachery and betrayal. It is the curse of the Fourcroys—"

But here the titter became outright laughter.

To hear this elderly man call the vibrant and dashing young Fourcroy his "uncle"! Well! That was too much for them, plainly.

The purple-eyed Fourcroy leaned forward and said something over the old man's head to the beautiful people in the front row (still beautiful! but Maya thought of the grains of earth already wriggling their way through Paris back to these smooth, unwrinkled faces and gave a satisfied shudder). In all the din Maya couldn't hear what the younger Fourcroy had to say, but two of the beautiful people stood up and reached out to take hold of the old Fourcroy's arms. The old man jumped when the strange hands touched him, and for a moment he seemed about to pitch right over.

"Hey," said James. "You're standing on my foot!"

Maya was cold with indignation and fury; there was

nothing else she could have done at that moment but rise up and move forward. But first she leaned down to James and put a stern finger in front of his face.

"You stay right here," she hissed. "And I mean it. Don't *move*. Don't make a *sound*. No matter what."

"What are you doing? I thought we were hiding."

"We are. You are, anyway. I just have to go yell at them all for a moment. Now *be quiet*."

And with one last warning glare, she scooted out from behind the crates and, keeping to the shadows, made her way right up to the edge of the gray curtain, up to the border between shade and brightness, hiding and not-hiding.

The old Fourcroy was flinging himself back and forth in the arms of his captors. Maya could catch only snatches of his angry, helpless words: "kidnapped," she thought she heard, and "Fourcroy," and even, perhaps, "*anbar*," but by this point, nobody was listening to him. The beautiful people in the audience were standing, peering forward, laughing, exclaiming. And the beautiful young Fourcroy stood very still, his dark hair very bright under the stage lights, his head bent slightly forward. Waiting for the disturbance to end.

Now, thought Maya. And then she stopped thinking at all for a second, and walked out from behind the curtain into the light.

It was like falling into a very bright sea. For a moment she could not really see anything at all but the light, and even all the noise in the theater seemed to change its quality as she stepped out onto that stage: She was encased in a bubble of light and very far away from everything else in the world. And then the bubble was gone, and there was noise and commotion all around. A few of those distant faces—and some pointing arms—were beginning to turn her way.

"Let go of that man!" she said, as loudly as she could.

Not too many people heard her at first, but the young Fourcroy turned slowly around and looked at her, an unreadable expression clouding his beautiful, purple eyes, and Maya could feel the shift in the audience, as people began to follow his gaze.

"I mean it: *Let go of him!*" she said again.

"And who might you be?" asked one of the beautiful people holding the poor old Fourcroy's arms twisted behind his back. The Old Man, at that same instant, looked up in his distress, and when he saw Maya standing there in the light above him, his angry face relaxed.

"Ah," he said. "It's Maya! My brave girl!"

But she was careful not to look too closely at him, not to let anything get in the way of her cold, hard rage.

"You let him go," she said to those beautiful people in as fierce a voice as she could muster. "He was the Keeper of the Cabinet of Earths. Don't you *dare* touch him."

There was a patchwork gasp from the audience: Some of the most beautiful people had heard of the Cabinet. They craned their necks to see better.

"Look at her, look at her," said the Old Man, twisting around to beam at the people nearest him. "A real Lavirotte! Finally a real Lavirotte!"

And that whisper began to spread through the crowd: *Lavirotte, Lavirotte!*

The young Fourcroy gave a quick signal with his head, and the beautiful people let go of the Old Man's arms.

"Perhaps he will go along with you, the poor old man," said the purple-eyed Fourcroy to Maya, his voice the very spirit of mildness. "Or you may stay, if you like, of course."

"To tell the truth, he came here because—I sent him," said Maya, and at that the hall fell completely silent.

"You, *mademoiselle*?" said the younger Fourcroy, with a thin-lipped smile. "You sent him to us? How unkind of you. He has been uncomfortable here, I'm afraid."

"Yes, I have!" shouted the Old Man from beyond the edge of the stage. "Because of your goons, my uncle, you fraudulent bag of pestilence!"

"I had to send him away from the Cabinet, you see," said Maya, pressing her arms against her sides to keep them from shaking. "So I could do what I had to do. I sent him here with a warning. Did you get it, I hope? To give my brother back. Or else!"

The purple-eyed Fourcroy laughed out loud, not a very nice laugh.

"You are a child from where? From America, I believe? Is this how children behave, then, in America?"

A couple of people in the audience followed his lead and laughed, but then the hush spread back over everything.

"The thing is, you don't really know who I am," said Maya. "I am a Lavirotte; it's true what he was saying. As well as being Maya Davidson. And one other thing—"

She pulled the green bottle out of her coat pocket and held it up so that the bright lights scattered greenly all around and the earth inside it seemed to writhe about.

"—I am also the new Keeper of the Cabinet of Earths," she said.

His face changed then: The color faded to something much paler. But when his hand whipped out to grab the bottle, she had already scooted to the left, just out of reach, and plucked the woolen sheep out of the neck of the bottle.

"And if you touch me, you see, I will throw this earth right into your face. Tell us all, Monsieur Fourcroy, what have you done to my brother?"

The purple-eyed Fourcroy froze, his eyes as fixed on

Maya and that bottle as if he were a snake trying to hypnotize its prey.

"I'm afraid you've lost your senses, *mademoiselle*," he said.

"Not me. I am here to *rescue* my brother," she said. "But *you* killed your brother during the war. The Old Man's father. *You* handed him over to the Nazis. And the people he was hiding in this building, you handed them over, too."

"If they had no business here," said the purple-eyed Fourcroy, "then why wouldn't I report them?"

"Well, that's disgusting," said Maya. "They were your cousins, too. That should count for something."

"Ah, now, but you're speaking of the war," he said. "That was very long ago, wasn't it? Just how old do you think I am?"

"I know exactly how old you are," said Maya. "You were born the year they built the Salamander House. Nineteen-oh-one."

The purple-eyed Fourcroy raised an eyebrow, and many of the people in the audience laughed a little. But the most beautiful, most perfect people sat silent.

"Listen," said Maya. "I've thought about this a lot, and it all has to stop. It's wrong. You take children who are happy and lucky, and you eat up their charm and their luck. You took my Cousin Louise, *you took my brother*, you took that old lady who sits outside on the bench—but oh, now I forget her name—"

"Amandine!" said a quavery old voice from the audience, but Maya was thinking of the right words to say and hardly noticed.

"I think I know what has done this to you. You locked up time in a Cabinet, and it made you cold. And careless. You just went on and on, living, until you forgot that other people aren't just your toys, aren't just creatures for you to use up to make your awful, addictive *anbar*. Perhaps if immortality wasn't—if it weren't—"

One of the most splendid women in the audience stood up at that moment, an elegant column rising right up out of the second row.

"Maya!" she said sternly. "Enough!"

Maya blinked. It was—it was—could it be?—

The woman made her way into the aisle and came striding toward the steps at the side of the stage.

"Your verbs are abominable. And worse: You have entirely lost control of your pronouns."

It was! An utterly transfigured Cousin Louise! Not younger, no—but so glowing, alluring, enchanting! What had she done to herself? Then Maya remembered the honey jar and felt her stomach turn to ice.

But she had only a moment to gape at the newly splendid Louise before she had to hop to the side again as the man before her made another swipe at the bottle.

"I see you have some of my property, *mademoiselle,*" he said, while she recovered her balance. "Be a good girl, now, and return it. And then we'll go find your brother, shall we? Because remember how we spoke of ambrosia, Maya? I have something very delicious, you know, for you to try."

"You mean this?" said Maya, bringing out the empty silk case from her pocket. "You mean this 'gift'? You mean, so I could be hooked on *anbar* like all the rest of them? And be guilty all my sparkly, beautiful life because you had fed me my own *brother*? And be addicted, and pathetic, and totally under your thumb? Is that what you mean? Because if it is—"

But at that moment a voice broke into her tirade: a sweet, arresting, and melodious voice, with the hint of a laugh just under its surface.

"Now, now, now, now . . ." said that voice. And Maya stopped short, aghast.

Cousin Louise came across the stage; under those tremendous lights she was so radiant, she seemed to glow with some inner light. The eyes of the audience were fixed on her. Maya herself could hardly look away. There was nothing invisible about this Cousin Louise! No, she was downright *compelling.* Charming. Glorious. And now the beautiful, radiant woman came right up to the side of the purple-eyed Fourcroy and rested a delicate hand, for a moment, against his arm.

"Give me a minute, *mon ami*," she said to him, in her low and newly thrilling voice. "She's a reasonable child. She'll listen to me."

Maya looked at them both as if from a tremendous distance. Her mind could not grasp any of this, but she could not take her eyes off of them. The purple-eyed Fourcroy was staring at Cousin Louise in dazed admiration; you could tell he didn't recognize her in her new, glorious self. But then, again, who would?

Cousin Louise turned to face Maya now.

"This man is the creator of *anbar*, you know, my dear."

"Yes," said Maya, the word just managing to struggle out somehow through her tense lips.

"And, ah, Maya, *anbar* is a quite remarkable substance, wouldn't you say?"

And for a moment Cousin Louise actually *preened*! Maya could say nothing at all; she just stood there and gaped.

"And now he would like his bottle back, *ma fille*. What do you think, my dear, shall we give him back his earths?"

Her voice was so soft and convincing; it seemed to want to reel its hearers right in. Maya stared at her in horror, half-transfixed by that voice and those eyes. Cousin

Louise, turned into one of the beautiful people! It was hard to fathom, really.

And then a thought came into her mind that was so terrible in every respect that Maya's heart quailed for a moment: Who was it, after all, who had put the *anbar* in that honey jar? No, there was no way around it, when you looked the thing squarely in the face: This disaster, too, was *all Maya's fault*.

Behind Cousin Louise she could just see the face of her cousin-uncle Fourcroy. He was beginning to smile. Cousin Louise smiled, too, brilliantly, entrancingly.

It was so hard to resist that voice, that musical, soothing voice. Maya shook herself a little, trying to recover some shred of stubbornness.

"You should know, though," she said, trying not to let her voice wobble even a bit. "The Cabinet of Earths—it doesn't even exist anymore. Not as it was, anyway. Look!"

And she pulled out the iridescent disk that hung from her neck on its bit of string and flashed it in her cousin-uncle's face.

"Here it is, your Cabinet of Earths! That's all that's left of it now—right there, that pretty piece of glass! It didn't save anybody, not really; it ruined them. So I destroyed it."

"Did you?" said the splendid Cousin Louise. (In the audience there were scattered exclamations, and out of the corner of her eye Maya saw a few people jump to their feet in alarm. But her attention was entirely on the radiant face before her.) "That was very hotheaded of you, *chérie*, wasn't it? But at least, as we can see, you saved this particular bottle. Good girl. It's the right thing to do—I know you know it. We must give your uncle back his earths. . . ."

And at that moment, as Maya searched in vain for some way to stand her ground against this beautiful, shining, corrupted version of Cousin Louise, the lid of one of those brilliant eyes made a sudden, lightning dip: a wink.

"Oh, but don't you do it, *ma fille*!" the old Fourcroy was shouting from his place at the foot of the stage. "They're no good, these people!"

Maya's arms figured it all out before her brain even got to the question. Before she could even ask herself what that wink might mean, the bottle was in the hands of the charming, terrifying Cousin Louise.

"All right, then," said Maya, her voice surprising her by sounding both quiet and calm. Inside her head, though, her thoughts were moving almost too quickly, jumping and shouting, tumbling all over the place. Somewhere, very far away, it seemed, there was a faint howl of frustration from someone, an old man's howl.

"Aha!" said Cousin Louise, whirling around to the purple-eyed Fourcroy. "Now you, my dear *monsieur*! Hold out your hands!"

And he did stretch out a hand, eagerness flickering in

every corner of his beautiful face.

Everywhere in that room, people sucked in their breath and held it. Maya's heart beat very fast—and then seemed to pause, waiting—

Cousin Louise smiled for a moment, her warm, new, alluring smile—and then in one swift motion tipped the old green bottle over, so that the earth came pouring out into the man's smooth hand.

"I am Louise Lavirotte Aron Marmier," she said, still smiling, but the smile was darker now, and terrifying. "One of the children, *monsieur*, whom you drained. But you see: We do not forget."

He shouted in surprise when the first clumps touched him. Horror and disbelief contorted his face for a moment, and then he put out his other hand, too, cupping them to catch as much of the earth as possible. It was very dark stuff, darker than coffee grounds, and it hissed slightly as it fell, hissed, and sank into his skin, leaving angry black streaks wherever it landed.

There was nothing Maya could have done; hardly even time enough to realize what was happening. She saw his face crumple and fold, his eyes fade, his hair lose its color, and the earth began spilling out of his hands onto the floor, where it evaporated with sizzles and pops. He gazed with alarm at the earth in his hands and then looked around for something, anything, to put it in, but there was nothing but the bottle, and that was still firmly in Cousin Louise's possession. And then a few moments later he was just a little old hunched-over man, an ancient little man, glaring up at them and muttering rude words under his breath while he stuffed handfuls of earth into his pockets.

The hush in the room had collapsed as soon as the earth started pouring into the man's hands, and now all around them the noise grew and grew. All of a sudden a low buzzing had entered the hall, as if a swarm of particularly tiny insects had finally reached the doors and slipped through them. Maya saw one or two of the beautiful people swat at something in the air around them; then a few others begin twisting about in alarm, as the first grains of earth reached their hands and their faces and began to work all the changes time always brings.

Oh, everywhere she looked now the beautiful people were crying out or slapping at their skin and the air or talking in frantic tones among themselves or even, some of them (the Dolphin's parents!), beginning to approach the stage, their lovely eyes full of loathing and fear. *They are going to eat us up now,* thought Maya incoherently. A little figure in the second row was just flinging back the great veil that had been wrapped around her bland face, a shrunken shadow of an old woman, still mousey but proud: the bag lady! And other people were standing up and shouting in confusion because they had just seen that beautiful young man with the purple eyes melt into something ancient and hobbled. "The bottle!" they were saying to one another. "Acid! Caustic! Assassin!" Angry, frightened words.

"You!" said the ancient little man right to Maya, while the chaos drowned everything out but the hatred in his voice and his eyes. "You idiot! You fool!" And then he turned away and shambled off to the side somewhere.

By then it was so loud in that hall that an old man's ravings didn't amount to very much; in fact, it was so loud that when the alarms began to wail, at first Maya hardly noticed. It just seemed like more shouting and shrieking. But then someone small came bounding across the stage to her and pulled happily on her arm.

"Maya! Maya! Look! It's the *police*!"

Nothing made James happier than sirens and police cars.

"Is that really our lost James?" said the splendid Cousin Louise. Tears were actually springing into her beautiful, expressive eyes. "Maya! Can it be? *Mon dieu!* But he looks almost unharmed!"

For a second or two James looked at this fancier version of Cousin Louise with interest, but more and more police were pouring into the room, followed finally by someone else he recognized and could wave at.

"Hey, look! That's our friend Valko," he said to Louise.

"Now we're all going to be arrested. Cool."

"I quite doubt anyone will arrest you," said Cousin Louise, dabbing at her eyes.

"Arrest us and throw us right into jail!" said James, undaunted. "But then I'll tell them all about it, how the chair was making me sick, and in a year or two they'll take the handcuffs off, probably."

Maya couldn't wait a moment longer; she grabbed at Cousin Louise's elbow. There was something she had to ask now, before the chaos rose and swallowed the stage they were standing on.

"Cousin Louise! How could you take that stuff?" she said. "You were behaving like one of them. I thought it had eaten *you*, the *anbar*!"

Cousin Louise looked at her with eyes that, despite being more beautiful than any ordinary eyes, were still full of all the most human sorts of things—sadness and affection and love.

"My dear Maya," she said. "When I heard he had taken your brother, I knew it was time. And even then, I swore: only once, and only for revenge. Some child was drained of its joy and its luck for that *anbar*. Revenge! Oh, I swore that with every gram I ate."

"But I had the bottle of earths," said Maya. "You could have just let me throw it at him, or something."

Cousin Louise shook her head so violently her hair

almost crackled in the light.

"Never!" she said. "*Non!* What sort of cousin must you think I am? Revenge is another kind of poison, *ma fille*. And I am old, and I have a very tough stomach. So!"

But then Valko, a grin of relief spread very wide across his face, was already bounding up onto the stage.

"I called the police," he said. "When I got your note. I called Cousin Louise, and then I worried about it for a while, and then I thought since it was kidnapping, really, I'd better call the police. Do you mind?"

James, more than anyone else, perhaps, did not mind. By the time they left that building, Maya's brother had gotten to tell his story a dozen times already: *Cocoa, chair, she rescued me!*

Never in all their investigations, however, did the police find any trace of this mysterious uncle who had offered James hot cocoa: Henri de Fourcroy had shuffled away through the doors and passages he knew better than anyone else, and by the time they came looking for him, he was gone.

17
THREE GRAINS OF EARTH

"Imagine that!" said Maya's father, rustling the newspaper a little in his hand. "They were running some sort of a kidnapping ring through that house near James's school—you know, the one where that fourth cousin seven times removed lives, or whatever he's supposed to be. And then there was a plague of bugs or something, too. They all came out of their theater looking like smallpox victims—that's what it says here, anyway."

"Really?" said her mother. "Maya, did you hear that? You should probably stay away from there for a while."

"He's gone now, anyway," said Maya. "I told you that."

"He had a scary chair," said James, looking up from a croissant. "I'm glad he got old and went away."

Their mother laughed.

"Over thirty, was he?" she said. "A real geezer. Too bad we can't all win makeovers or some such, like Cousin Louise."

"No kidding!" said their father. "Nearly fell off my

chair when I first saw *her*."

Because it turns out that even when you try to tell your parents the truth, they hear what they want to hear, or what they're capable of hearing. Maya tried very hard with her own parents, but all the talk of *anbar* and Cabinets and mortalities kept in bottles just washed right over their heads and away.

Oh, well! Maya took a thoughtful bite of her croissant, just as the faint click of the dining room clock finally managed to catch her attention.

"Shoot!" she said, and jumped up. In five minutes the bell at the *collège* would ring and the gates swing shut. "I'm late *again*! Hey, did somebody do something with my schoolbag?"

"*I-do-on't-have-school, To-day-is-a-Wednes-day*," sang James under his breath. There, what's more, was her bag: hanging smugly on the back of her chair. It wasn't even worth it, pausing to frown at her brother. She was too busy with her jacket just then, squeezing her arms into the sleeves while stumbling toward the hall.

"Oh, right, and I'm going to be home a little late afterward," she said, remembering just in time. "I thought I might take Valko over to see the old Fourcroy today. The nice one. With the sets."

"Seventh cousin four times removed?" said her father.

"He's moving to the coast," said Maya. "He's going to

find a little shop somewhere, he says, in plain sight of the sea, and he's going to live there and make dollhouses."

"Lovely!" said Maya's mother. "Good for him!"

"Ooh, he's the one Maya broke the cabinet of," said James. "I never get to break things. It's not fair."

Their parents paid no attention to him. Only Maya shot him a sharp glance. She still wondered sometimes how many drops of charm had been left behind in the tubing in the Salamander House. Couldn't be very many. But now, it was true, James could walk through a crowded store and not every head would turn. "Doesn't James seem a little older, somehow?" Maya's mother had said just the other day, with a sigh. "Must be the French schools."

It gave Maya's heart such a pang this morning that she ran all the way back to the table, bell or no bell, to give him a last-minute sisterly hug.

It had all worked out all right in the end, right? Her brother was safe and mostly fine, the purple-eyed Fourcroy was gone, the Cabinet no longer holding anyone under its spell. One day this week she had even seen Eugène de Raousset-Boulbon sitting at an ordinary, everyday restaurant table with his no-longer-so-young parents, so that was all right. But still she felt a little restless inside, just the slightest bit sad and loose-endish.

There had been that evening when Maya's mother had

come in to kiss her good night, and Maya had suddenly found it hard, hard, hard to let her go.

"Do you *really* not mind, not living forever and ever?" she had said into her mother's ear. "I could have saved you, putting a bottle for you in the Cabinet of Earths. Do you really not mind?"

"Oh, Maya, what is it with you and those bottles?" her mother had said, but she had hugged Maya very tightly all the same. "People can't be saved in jars! Think how boring! Never changing!"

But sometimes that's exactly what a person wants, isn't it? A world with *no change.*

She hadn't meant to say anything about it to Valko, but he took a sideways look at her after school and suggested they take their sandwiches out to their favorite bench in the park (past the Fountain of Lost Children, where the sad cherubs were pondering the mound of bouquets left at their feet by sentimental people after the events of the weekend: *Stéphane*, 1961; *Juliette*, 1962—all of them "lost," after all, as it turned out, since how could anyone really find you again, once you had been drained of your charm, your appeal, your *anbar*?). And then somehow after the sandwiches were gone, they ended up doing a long lap around the park while the late October sun got thinner and thinner. Just talking it all over one more time.

And by the time they came to the end of the story and

looked up from the sidewalk, there they were again, at the door of the Salamander House.

"He's gone now," said Valko, misreading Maya's shiver, which was really at least 60 percent due to the wind. "Can't cause you any more trouble."

"The way he withered up when the earth touched him," said Maya, and she hugged her jacket close to her sides. "All his beautifulness just withered right away."

"Caustic stuff," said Valko. "Wonder what it really was, in that bottle. Not ordinary earth, obviously. I used to have this huge chemistry set, years ago: holes in the carpet and puffs of smoke. My mom threw it out one day when I was at school."

But he stopped and gave Maya another look, a quieter, warmer look than you might have expected from all those words, so she decided not to be too discouraged by the chemistry set.

"Earth," she said again firmly. "It's what mortality looks like, extracted."

"Well," said Valko, in his diplomatic way, "*something* happened to that awful man. That's for sure."

The wind picked up just then; even the brass salamander on the door looked like it wanted to be somewhere else, somewhere warmer, a place where it could curl up like a cat on a hearth. Maya wrapped her arms more tightly around herself and shivered again.

"They still had the Alchemical Theater all blocked off the last time I was here," said Valko. "Not to mention crawling with police."

But when they moved down the sidewalk to take a look, there was no one there at all, just long strands of police tape fluttering in the wind.

"Bet they're off having lunch," said Valko. "Or carting more evidence away."

They stood there for a moment, just looking at the dead leaves eddying on the theater steps. Then Valko made a tiny motion with his feet, a well-maybe-we-should-keep-moving-on sort of gesture. Which made perfect sense, considering the temperature of the air.

"Wait a sec," said Maya. She was trying to figure something out. Namely: Why did she suddenly need to duck under that police tape and climb up to the theater's door?

"What are you doing?" said Valko.

But he followed her, all the same. Ducking under police tape was really much more Valko's cup of tea than Maya's, under most circumstances.

"I think I must have left something in there," said Maya as she put her hand on the door. "Why can't I remember what?"

And the door wasn't even locked.

Inside the hall the air was very dim. Oval glints of

glass from the doors leading into the theater proper. And through those doors, a cave of darkness where that bright, bright theater had been.

"Hm," said Valko, and she heard him rustling through the pockets of his backpack. But she was trying very hard to put her finger—to put her mind's finger—on that missing thing, whatever it was, that had been haunting her all day. All week. In fact, since that terrible Saturday—

And then she knew what it was she was looking for, stumbling all zombie-like down the dark aisles of the Alchemical Theater.

The *hourglass.*

"There!" said Valko, some steps behind her, and a little puddle of yellow light started wobbling along the floor in front of her feet. He had found his flashlight. "Ever since the power went out at the embassy that night, I've kept a—"

"Hurry," said Maya, interrupting. "There's a door at the back of the stage."

The flashlight made the rest of the dark even darker. Shadows everywhere.

"This is a little bit nuts," said Valko. He sounded quite cheerful about it, though. "Where are we going?"

"Back here," said Maya. "Oh, watch out, there's more of that tape. Wait."

She wriggled her way past the tape and through that

other door. And in this part of the theater, the darkness became something almost solid. Valko's flashlight couldn't do much against it, just flicked to the right and left. More doors. Except for their breathing and the soft scuffing noises their careful feet made against the floorboards, there was no sound in this part of the theater. None whatsoever.

"It's that one," said Maya in a whisper, waving her arm toward the left end of the hall. "I remember now. Quick!"

She practically ran to that door, pushed it open even ahead of Valko's dim light, and then stood there, looking from one sort of darkness into another. The round room. The tree. She just felt it all there in the dark, as if it had been waiting a very long time for them to arrive.

"Whoa," said Valko, turning his flashlight this way and that. A glimpse of carved branches, the glint of amber eyes, the backs of those benches, more police tape—she couldn't see properly from here.

"Watch out, there are steps," said Maya as she felt her way down toward the center, where the trunk was. It was hard to see, because of the tape.

It was hard to see—because behind the tape, nothing was there.

"Turn that light off!" said Maya in distress. The light must be tricking her eyes.

"Really?" said Valko, but there was a click, and the room tumbled into blackness.

Maya felt forward with her hands, found the stump of the tree, yes, but where the hourglass had been—nothing. Her hands were as blind as her eyes.

The hourglass was gone.

And all that vague sense of loss that had been sloshing around inside her since that Saturday coalesced around this one plain fact: The hourglass was no longer there.

"It's gone," she said helplessly into the empty dark. "Where'd it go?"

"Hey, Maya," said Valko. "Look up."

It wasn't so completely dark, after all. There were tiny stars above their heads, peeking through the branches of the wooden tree. Pointless, glittering stars.

"Valko, *listen*. There was an hourglass here, before," said Maya. "I've got to get it back. It stole my earth."

Valko flicked the flashlight back on, and the darkness instantly rearranged itself yet again: shadows everywhere.

"You want some old hourglass that's been carted off by the evidence guys?"

"I want my earth back," said Maya. "It has three grains of my earth. That's what I want back."

There was a pause.

"Explain how you're figuring this," said Valko.

"I was in this room, that Saturday! I was tricked somehow. I put my hands on the hourglass, and it sucked the earth right out of me. Not a lot of it. But still. I want it back."

"Because—?"

Because it was supposed to be for her mother, if anybody, that hourglass. So her mother could have been safe and well, not just for now, but forever and ever. It was like an ache that wouldn't let up, having to let go of that dream. And it was awful to think that the only mortality salted away, after all of that, was just some tiny part of Maya's own.

And those weren't even the only reasons. She gritted her teeth.

"Those awful people!" she said. "The Dolphin's awful parents! You may not care, but I do. I don't want to turn into *that*, with all the earth sucked out of me. I mean, I didn't lose much of it, really. Three grains! Nothing! But what those people were willing to do to James! What they did to Cousin Louise! That terrible Uncle Fourcroy with his terrible eyes—"

—What was it that happened then?

Almost nothing.

The tiniest of rustles, off in a corner. The shadows shifting ever so slightly. Or maybe it was just Valko's flashlight, flickering for a moment because the battery was not really very new. But whatever it was, the whole world changed.

In that instant they both became very aware of certain things, like the fact they were in a dark, dark room in a building filled with shadows. They weren't supposed to be there, nobody knew they were in there, they were completely alone, and something was rustling in the corner.

They looked at each other, turned, and skedaddled, not even caring anymore about the noise their feet made against the floor, or the way their elbows and shins kept banging into walls, doors, the backs of chairs. They didn't stop until they were out again on the sidewalk in front of the theater, their lungs sobbing for air and their hearts thumping like crazy.

"And *oops*," said Valko, raising his head just for a millisecond. "Here comes the police."

Indeed, a *gendarme* was just at that very moment wheeling around the corner, coming back to his post from wherever he'd been. He took one frowning look at Valko and Maya and warned them away from the steps with a crisp wave of his hands.

"Allez-vous en," said the policeman. "Off you go. Nothing to see here."

As soon as they were out of the policeman's sight, Maya and Valko had to lean against the wall for a moment, caught somewhere between gasping for breath and laughter.

"What *was* that in there?"

"A rat, I guess."

"The shadow of a rat!"

"Policeman almost caught us."

"One half second later—"

For a time they hardly even noticed the chill in the air. But then they had caught their breaths again, and Valko took her hand and gave it a comforting squeeze.

"Well, now you know, anyway," he said. "Your hourglass is gone. It's probably wrapped in seven layers of plastic on a shelf in the back room of the Préfecture de Police. No one will ever see it again."

"I just wanted my earth back," said Maya.

Valko looked like someone imagining what a police secretary might say, if a couple of kids came up to her counter and asked for *three grains of earth, left by accident in an hourglass.* He opened his mouth and snapped it shut again.

"What?" said Maya.

"What do you mean, *what*?" said Valko, innocently. "And what's that you're wearing?"

It was the shiny disk of Cabinet glass on its string; it must have slipped out of her jacket when they were running away from that shadow in the theater. She showed him its tricks, how it could melt in her hand if she asked it to, and then in another blink of an eye be solid again.

"Very cool," said Valko. "What's it made of, anyway?"

And he poked a finger at it, but the disk almost seemed to flinch away; at any rate, his hand couldn't grasp it.

"It's shy," said Maya.

"Shy!" said Valko. "Necklaces aren't *shy*!"

But his eyes were all alive with scientific interest.

"Can't be mercury," he said. "It's transparent. And what's that thing in it?"

It was true, there was something there, trapped in the glass. Why hadn't she noticed that before? A narrow speck of darkness, like a question mark, like a microscopic creature caught in a drop of water on a slide.

It was,

in fact,

the tiniest of salamanders.

And it looked up over its shoulder at them, looked over its shoulder and flicked its tail.

They watched it for a moment in silence, and then Maya tucked the disk of glass away, a warm mysterious circle against the bottom of her throat.

"A trick of the light," said Valko, shaking his head with a smile.

A little bit of Lavirotte in me, thought Maya, and something in her heart fell comfortably into place.

Because some people are like that: They live in more worlds than one.

They may have dogs and friends and a wonderful, ordinary life in some wonderful, ordinary town far away—and yet in Paris they can find themselves walking in magic.

And that, in the end, is the nature of salamanders:

Salamanders are amphibious.

AUTHOR'S NOTE

This story is also, like its heroine, a little bit amphibious. Everything that happens is fictional, as are all of the main characters, but some of the people and places mentioned are real. Antoine François Fourcroy (1755–1809) and Antoine-Laurent Lavoisier (1743–1794) were both chemists in France in the eighteenth century. They worked together for many years, and after Lavoisier was sent to the guillotine during the French Revolution, Fourcroy (who was part of the Revolutionary government) was widely accused of having played a role in Lavoisier's death—or at least not doing much to save the man who had been his mentor for so long.

There are some excellent books about Lavoisier, who really did have an interest in everything from guinea pigs to sheepfolding: I recommend *Antoine Lavoisier: Founder of Modern Chemistry* (Great Minds of Science), by Lisa Yount (Enslow Publishers, 1997), for a good introduction. The book I got the guinea pig story from (and so much else besides) is a wonderful biography by Douglas McKie: *Antoine Lavoisier: Scientist, Economist, Social Reformer* (New York: Henry Schuman, 1952).

The painting in the Louvre Museum that Maya's mother loves so much was painted by Jan van Eyck around 1435 and is called *The Madonna of Chancellor Rolin.* Look closely, and you will see the island of the Lavirottes!

And if you are lucky enough to find yourself in Paris, do try to get to 29 avenue Rapp. There is a house there you might recognize—and it really does have a bronze salamander on its door.

ACKNOWLEDGMENTS

No book ever had better friends than this one. Its editor, Rosemary Brosnan, is my hero. She read each revision with a gimlet eye and a kind heart: Madeleine L'Engle would have called her a Teacher.

Present at this story's birth were some particularly generous and inspirational Parisian godmothers—Tioka Tokedira, Sarah Towle, Michèle Helene, and Emma Pearson Groleau. They read the earliest drafts with wise, writerly eyes, and I am deeply grateful to them.

Sharon Inkelas, Will Waters, and Jayne Williams have been the truest of friends, not just to this book (which wouldn't be itself without them), but also to the author, whose breath is taken away time and time again by their patience, their support, and their love.

At a critical moment, Andrea Brown came aboard to pilot the book into safe harbor. Mary Kole, Lee Naiman, and Kathleen Duey saw early versions of the story and gave sage advice. Marguerite Holloway encouraged me. My tolerant colleagues in Slavic and Film have been as tickled by my interest in magical salamanders as any colleagues could possibly be.

Marie-José Hadifé is the true Keeper of the Cabinet of Earths and the kindest of hosts; she taught us some wonderful lessons about the nature of desert glass and how to treat bee stings.

My world wouldn't be the same without my sisters: Barbara Nesbet made me the most beautiful salamander quilt when I finished this book, and Susan Nesbet Sikuta was always the one who found the best library books when we were kids—I hope Caroline likes this one!

My mother, Helen MacPherson Nesbet, would have been thrilled to see this story in print, and doubly thrilled to read the bit about a mother dragging a kid to the Louvre. I miss her. Thanks to her and to my physicist father, Robert Nesbet, I know all too well what it feels like to be popped into schools where no one speaks your language.

Eric Naiman has strange ideas about what should go into a book, but he is the best possible person with whom to explore the world's odd corners. Thera Naiman, Eleanor Naiman, Ada Naiman, and Jenna Archer made life in Paris complete: This book is dedicated, with love and gratitude, to them.